FOR THE POWER

Debbie Cassidy

CONTENTS

Chapter One

The road ahead had once been a motorway but was now overgrown and littered with stationary vehicles. Ash steered the van expertly between them, and up ahead Jace wove between the cars with ease on his motorbike. Logan snoozed on a mattress in the back of the van while my eyes scanned the road for possible trouble, but at this speed, in the daytime, we should be safe from the Feral.

We'd been on the road for a couple of hours and were getting closer to the coordinates for the first bunker, but we'd have to go off road to get to it. Another half hour and then we'd have to go on foot. We'd made sure to leave early to ensure we reached the bunker in good time, to ensure that if something went wrong we had enough time to find shelter for the night.

It was strange traveling during the day when Tobias and I had spent so long with the moon as our guide, running, always running. It was strange not to have a knot of tension the size of a grapefruit in my chest.

Tobias's face came to mind, his lopsided grin and sparkling green eyes. The way he always knew what to say to defuse a situation. The way he'd held me when we'd finally fallen asleep at dawn, managing to make me feel safe even though the world waited to swallow us alive.

I'd failed him.

I'd failed to get him away from the Feral. I'd allowed the Vladul to have him and now I was driving in the opposite direction from where he was.

For the cure, Eva. You're doing this for the cure. Dad's voice in my head again, reminding me of my purpose. Of the mission, the goal, the be all and end all of it all, and yes, Tobias would understand.

Ash's hand cupped my knee and squeezed before settling back on the steering wheel. I glanced across at him, at his sturdy profile, the slope of his nose and the slight pout of his beautiful lips. He'd cut his hair before we left, shoring it down so it was a golden buzz cut. It accentuated his stone-cut features.

Ogre … yeah, I could see the strength in the

lines of his body, the bulk of his biceps, and the bulge of his thighs as he shifted gears and pressed down on the accelerator. But the word *ogre* brought to mind an ugly, monstrous creature, and Ash was anything but ugly. His features were brutal, yes, but there was a compelling symmetry to his makeup, and an undeniable charisma to his presence even though he never uttered a word.

"Like the scenery, Eva?" Logan drawled from the back of the van.

"Great, you're awake." My tone was pure sarcasm.

Logan chuckled. "I've got to give it to you, you don't faze easily—no pretty blush, no embarrassment at being caught ogling."

Wrong, so wrong. I was just good at hiding my embarrassment, but he didn't need to know that. "Oh, dear, are you jealous I wasn't ogling you?"

Ash didn't take his eyes off the road, but the corner of his mouth curled up slightly, telling me he was tuning into the conversation.

Logan let out a sharp bark of laughter. "Oh, honey, you couldn't handle this."

"I wouldn't want to."

The satcom radio on the dashboard crackled, and Noah's voice filled the van. "How's it going? Over."

I lifted the radio and pressed down on the button. "We're almost ready to go off road. Over."

"Good. It should be quiet in the daytime. Call me when you reach the bunker. Over."

Logan's breath was hot on my cheek. He reached for the radio, and I let him have it, but he hung between the seats, his body too close, his scent too strong. "How's Gina? Is everything okay on your end? Over."

Like he cared. I focused on the road ahead.

"She's fine, Logan. We're fine. Call in when you get to the bunker. Over and out."

The radio went dead. Logan threw it into my lap and then retreated into the back of the van again. Noah had sounded almost curt when speaking to Logan; there was definitely tension between them, and something that Jace had alluded to came to mind. Something that suggested that Logan had a reason to have issues with Noah. The Fangs had secrets that I'd probably never uncover and that shouldn't bother me. They weren't my problem, they were a temporary stop in my journey, they were a convenient helping hand to get to where I needed to be. This was an alliance that was necessary to save us all.

Heck, who was I kidding, secrets bugged me. Not knowing bugged me. Not fully understanding their dynamic was like an annoying splinter, but instinct warned me that the direct approach of simply asking was out of the question in this case.

I propped the radio back in its spot on the dash. It would keep us tethered to Noah on this long trip, because unlike regular radios, it used satellites in space to bounce signals. Tech stuff I didn't completely understand, but Noah had explained the bunker still had access to the satellites in space, and he tapped into the correct frequency to make sure the satcom worked.

Up ahead, Jace revved his engine, flying ahead of us. We'd barely spoken this morning. The awkwardness after he'd almost allowed Logan to drain me dry still hovered between us, and when he'd said he'd be riding his bike there was no denying the relief I'd felt. It didn't matter; though; this relationship was a partnership, not a friendship. We were all here for the cure, and they'd protect me for as long as it took to get it. They'd protect me for as long as they needed my blood.

Cynical much?

I ignored the inner voice because this wasn't Dad. This was the suppressed part of me that liked to make connections. The part that had decided Tobias couldn't be left behind, and the part that had been overridden by pure instinct under the bridge when the monster had been about to devour us.

They kept Gina around even though she's infected.

5

Maybe it's not all about the blood. Maybe it could be about friendship. The cure is out there. You did what you were supposed to. No need to keep the walls up.

It was right, but the thoughts sent fear shooting through me. To open up and make friends, to let people in, to care meant the possibility of loss and pain and grief.

But if we cure the world …

Yeah, if we cure the world.

Ash turned his head sharply to look at me, a question on his face. I shook my head and fixed my gaze on the road, on Jace's weaving form, and pursed my lips. Of course he could sense my fear, the spike in my adrenaline. But he had gone back to eyes-on-the-road mode now, thank goodness.

"What are you afraid of, Eva?" Logan asked casually from the back of the van.

Damn Fangs and their extrasensory abilities. "Nothing."

"Liar."

Up ahead, Jace's bike swerved sharply to the left, toppled to the side, and skidded along the ground. My hands slapped the dash, and a cry fell from my lips. Ash accelerated. But Jace was off his bike, waving his arms in the air and jumping up and down, lips moving in warning.

"What? What was he saying?"

And then my gaze fell on the thing glinting in the middle of the road—a chain of barbs.

I grabbed at Ash's bicep. "Watch out!"

He slammed on the brakes, but the van was going too fast. We weren't going to avoid it. We weren't going to—

Several loud pops and bangs assaulted my ears and then the van swerved sharply to the right, whiplashing my head to the side and jarring my teeth. The seatbelt snapped taut, slamming me back into the seat and holding me there.

"The fuck?" Logan moaned from the back of the van.

Shit, he didn't have a belt. I unsnapped mine and made to climb into the back to help him, but Ash grabbed my arm, his eyes on the road ahead.

"What?" I tracked his gaze and froze.

Jace was no longer alone. He was surrounded by huge, powerful-looking guys carrying clubs, axes, and in a couple of cases, machetes. Shaved heads and square jaws greeted us, their amber eyes glowing bright in their faces.

Logan's breath tickled the side of my face. "Fuck this, we can take them."

He was right. There were eight of them and four of us. Easy pickings.

I reached for the sword and sheath at my feet. "Let's do this."

Ash unbuckled his seatbelt and reached for the door release just as several more figures poured onto the road around us.

Logan cursed softly.

"Or maybe not?"

Chapter Two

TOBIAS

I ncessant soft sobs filled the room, drifting from between the bars and rising like mournful, invisible smoke. There was something about the sound of a woman's sobs that needled at my heart and stabbed at my gut—not as motivating as a child's or baby's cry but terrible nonetheless.

The sense of impotency grated. No words helped, and physical comfort was restricted by the bars between us all. There was no choice but to tune it out. Fear, desperation, and hopelessness tainted the air in an aroma of devastation.

At least the cells our captors had herded us into were clinically clean. My skin smelled fresh for the first time in ages, kissed by crisp cotton pants and a T-shirt, an outfit which contrasted sharply with the white floors, walls, and ceiling.

We were black smudges against a clinical background. We were food that had been cleansed and wrapped in fresh packaging, ready for consumption. We'd even been fed a sloppy gruel that had been surprisingly filling and tasty. Probably loaded with all the necessary protein and nutrients to keep us fit and healthy.

This was a holding bay—I'd heard the Fangs who'd herded us into the chamber talking about it when they'd propelled us into the cells, prodding us into action with black electrified batons. These were uninfected, strange-looking Fangs that shared common physical characteristics of pale skin and silver hair. Their faces were regal, bodies lithe and powerful, and they intended to keep us alive. It was obvious by the way they were treating us.

See, Eva, I was listening and paying attention in class.

Eva … Her face when they'd driven off with me. The devastation. She'd come for me, it had been in her eyes, in the set of her jaw. Part of me reveled in this knowledge and the other part despaired, because this place was a fortress, and not even Eva, with her skills and her wonderful mind, would be able to penetrate it.

Was it a blessing to live, even if it meant being caged and tapped for blood, or would it have been better to have died in the Feral den? The thought circled my mind like a vulture.

Emily would have chosen life. The desire to live had blazed in her eyes when the Feral had come for her, dragging her from the room kicking and screaming. She hadn't come back.

Life meant hope, no matter how tenuous. I gripped the bars and studied my surroundings one more time. It was what Eva would do. She'd file the details in that beautiful mind of hers, looking for a way out, a breach, something she could exploit later. But the room was bare except for the cells and the black-clad humans inside. There was only one exit —a steel door with a red bulb above it. They'd brought us in via that door and no doubt would take us out via it.

"I don't want to die," the woman in the cell next to mine whimpered.

Her long dark hair was still damp from the showers they'd shoved us into on arrival. The sting of hot water was a sensory memory still pricking my skin.

"Please. I don't want to die," she repeated.

"Shut the fuck up," someone snarled. "You think any of us want to die?"

No. No one here wanted to die, and I doubt our captors wanted us dead either. We were their source of food, their chance at survival. There weren't many uninfected humans remaining in the world, and they'd take care of us because they needed us.

Cameras dotted the crease between wall and ceiling. They were keeping an eye on us all right.

The woman in the cell next to mine hurled herself at the bars, slamming her head off the metal again and again. Blood bloomed to life on her forehead and her screams tore through the air. Adrenaline flooded me with the need to do something, but she was too far out of reach and losing it. From the way she was attacking the bars with her skull, it looked like she wasn't so eager to live after all.

The door opened with a beep and two silver-haired Fangs strode in — a male and a female. They made a beeline for the woman's cell, and the male raised a baton, ready to shove it between the bars. It would shock the woman into compliance.

My fingers and toes had tingled for an hour after they'd used one of those on me. *Time to back up out of the way, no touching the bars unless you want another shock.* Eva's voice was clear as a bell in my mind.

I backed up, but before the baton could make contact with the woman, the female Fang raised a hand to halt the male. She stepped up to the bars and wrapped her hand around the spot the woman was using to bash her own brains in.

The next blow glanced off the Fang's fingers, and the distraught woman froze and stared at the Fang in confusion.

The Fang smiled, showcasing lethal eyeteeth, another difference between the Feral and these Fangs. The Feral had elongated canines, which told me that this breed of Fang was different from the breed that had turned Feral. These Fangs were different in too many ways.

"Self-harm will not be tolerated," the Fang said evenly. "We do not wish to hurt you. You have something we need, and if you cooperate then no harm will come to you. Act out and there will be consequences."

The human woman's face contorted. "Fuck you, Fang." She hawked and spat in the Fang's face.

The globule of spittle landed on the Fang's cheek and then slowly dripped down her face. The Fang blinked impassively at the human and then moved so fast my eyes struggled to track the movement. There was a glint of silver and then the cell-bound woman was gurgling and thrashing about. A crimson line decorated her neck and blood welled up out of her mouth. Her eyes rolled back in her head, and she hit the ground. The white interior was suddenly silent and streaked with crimson.

The male Fang closed his eyes and inhaled.

"Get rid of it," the female said. While the male busied himself entering the cell to extract the dead body, she turned to the rest of us. "Let that be an example to you. Resist and you will die. Cooperate and you will live long, comfortable lives. Your bloodwork is being completed as we speak and then you'll be taken to your forever homes. You may even be reunited with your loved ones. Happy humans make for tastier blood." Her smile was matter-of-fact. "You'll be taken care of, fed, and given the opportunity to exercise; there is even an entertainment room. You'll be safe, and in exchange, you will feed us. Do you understand?"

There were several choruses of yes.

She inclined her head. "Good." Her gaze fell on me, lingering briefly.

I met her attention, unflinching. Show no fear, Eva would say. No fear.

Her lips curled in a satisfied smile, and then she turned on her heel and clipped from the room.

There was silence, deathly and complete, in her wake.

No more sobs drifted up to fill the air.

THEY CAME the next morning—three Fangs dressed in black from head to foot. They could have been one of us if not for their stature and the eerie silver hair. Cell doors were flung open and humans were herded out. No one protested. No one fought. And then they were gone. Everyone but me and two other guys. One was in a cell opposite and three down—blond and wiry but tall. His green eyes spoke of pain. The other was on the same side as me, four cells down, and now that the other cells were empty it was easy to get a good look at him. He was huge—Fang huge—with dark hair and a brooding demeanor. We exchanged confused glances.

"You think they forgot about us?" the blond asked.

"I doubt it," the dark-haired one said. "I figure they have something else in store for us."

My gut told me he was right, and we didn't have too long to wait before our suspicions were confirmed. The door beeped open five minutes later and two Fangs wearing white lab coats strode in. They stopped in front of my cell, studying me as if I was a specimen on display, which I guess I was.

"What is this?" blond guy asked. "Why are we still here when you took everyone else?" His tone was aggressive, his stance confrontational.

Don't engage, Eva warned. *You don't want to end up with a slit throat.*

She was right, there was no point aggravating

these Fangs, not when they had all the power and could kill us for defiance.

The Fangs didn't pay blondie any mind, though. Instead, they made notes on their clipboards, pausing to glance at the main door every few seconds.

They were waiting for someone.

And then the door opened again and the female Fang from earlier entered the room. Her pale skin blended well with the white lab coat she was sporting, but it made her dark eyes seem even darker, like two bottomless pits in her oval face. Those pits raked over me, then flicked to blond guy, and finally settled on dark-haired dude.

"What are you?" Blond guy practically spat the words. "What the fuck are you? You're not the usual Fangs. We have a right to know!"

Man, he had a death wish, but instead of getting annoyed, the female smiled widely, showing the first flash of real emotion. Satisfaction.

"Aggressive little thing, aren't you?" She canted her head. "It will serve you well on the path that has been chosen for you."

"That doesn't answer my question," blondie retorted.

"No. It doesn't, and I suppose there's no harm in satisfying your curiosity since you will be serving us very well in a short space of time. We aren't Fangs, little human. We are what Fangs evolved from. We are the first, we are the original, we are Vladul, and this world now belongs to us." Her smile was like a dagger. "Congratulations. You three have been selected to be modified. Welcome to Genesis."

Chapter Three

The glowing-eyed figures surrounded the vehicle. They moved quickly, efficiently cutting off all escape. Not that we'd be able to shoot off with flat tires and no Jace. One figure strode to the front of our van and placed a hand on the hood of the vehicle. He was broad-faced with high cheekbones and full lips. Several hoop earrings dangled from his lobes, and his defined biceps were bare in his vest shirt. A machete was strapped to his waist, dirty and crusted with dried blood.

"Don't do anything stupid," he said.

His voice carried easily, deep-timbred and smooth. His gaze flicked from me to Logan to Ash and then back again.

"The female will exit the vehicle first." It was a demand.

Right, they assumed if they had me in their grasp there was less chance of the guys fighting them. I bit back a smirk—oh ye of little faith, oh ye of underestimating the female race and their ability to wield a lethal weapon.

My sword was out of sight for them, but very much within my grasp. My fingers curled around the hilt.

"No." Logan's voice was low. "Don't try anything. Just do as he says."

I shot him an irritated glance. "Seriously?"

"Your sword won't do anything to them, all you'll do is murder the host."

"Host?"

"They're djinn, Eva, and the meat suits they're wearing are innocent humans."

My heart stalled for a moment. Djinn? As in the creatures made of smokeless fire that had hovered on the edges of human society for all time? They'd existed on a parallel plane and hungered for our world for as long as we'd laid claim to it. Dad had said they'd retreated to their world once the virus hit, but I guess, just like the fey, some had become trapped here. But taking human hosts... That wasn't something Dad had filled me in on. He'd explained how they were incorporeal on our plane but corporeal on their own, something to do with frequencies and light waves. I was no scientist.

"Just get out of the car. Don't fight them," Logan instructed.

Ash nodded in agreement.

Fine. Using my sword was a no, but that didn't mean I'd leave it behind. My passenger side door popped open, and I hopped out of the van with the sword and sheath held lightly in my hand. The djinn closest to the door stepped back to allow me room to exit. He looked down his nose at me as if I were a gnat, and a prickle ran over my skin at his proximity. Magic, sharp and tangy, hovered in the air. It was seeping from his pores and stroking my skin.

I arched a brow. "Hello to you too."

I brushed past him, suppressing a shudder, and strode to the front of the vehicle. My gaze grazed Jace's, and his frown told me all I needed to know.

This was not good.

The djinn who'd instructed me to get out of the van was studying me now, his brow furrowed in confusion. There was something about his face that was strangely arresting, and I had to force myself to stop staring only to note that he was watching me with an equal measure of intensity.

It was disconcerting, but there was no way he'd know he was throwing me off. "What? You've never seen a human female before?"

His glowing peepers dimmed to flame colored—hues of orange and red and flecks of deep blue—as he continued to eye-probe me.

"I've seen plenty of human females in my time," he said. "But none quite like you."

It sounded like an awful pick-up line, but his tone suggested otherwise. "Look, we don't want any trouble, we just want to be on our way."

He inclined his head. "And you can, but the vehicles and any tech you may be carrying stay with us."

"Wait ... This is a robbery?"

He grinned, showcasing even white teeth. "Ah, such a negative word." He spread his hands. "We like to call it basic acquisitions."

Was that a twinkle in his eye? Was he playing with me? The tension gripping me eased a bit as instinct told me that despite his massive frame, maybe this djinn didn't mean us any harm.

I looked to Ash. "They just want the van and bike." It was a loss. Yes, but we would have left them behind for the next stretch of the journey anyway. Granted, we'd planned on picking them up on the way back, but ... "We should just leave them and get going." I looked to the djinn for confirmation, but he was frowning now.

"What?"

He shook his head. "You misunderstand me. *You*

get to leave. The Fangs stay. The Fangs die." His lip curled in evident disgust.

A few days ago, I'd happily have dumped the Fangs in the shit and strolled off into the sunset, but they were no longer just Fangs to me. They were Jace and Ash and yeah, even Logan. They had stories and secrets and we'd shed blood together.

I held up my hands. "Whoa, wait up. If you want the van and bike, then that's cool. But the Fangs belong to me. I need them and you're not taking them." I met the djinn's gaze levelly.

His brows shot up. "*Belong* to you?"

It was a strong word, but it didn't feel like a lie. I lifted my chin. "Yeah. They're mine. If you want them, you're going to have to go through me."

I expected him to laugh, to look down his nose at me, but something akin to doubt flashed across his stony features. "You'd fight me for these blood-suckers? These creatures that feed on human life blood?"

Fuck, it sounded awful when he put it that way. "And how is taking human hosts any better?"

He stared at me flatly.

"Look, they're not like the Vladul or the Feral. They're victims just like us, and they saved my life several times." The details of our mission and the cure were on the tip of my tongue, but I bit them back. We didn't know what the djinn's agenda was, and the cure was too important to risk. "I *need* them."

He seemed to consider this, but then his expression closed off, and he stood tall. "I'm sorry, they're uninfected Fangs and we can't risk the Vladul getting hold of them and reinforcing their ranks. We've killed off two Feral dens and a brood of uninfected Fangs in the past two months. It's the only way to ensure the Vladul's numbers stay manageable."

"The last thing we want to do is join the Vladul," Jace said.

"If they get hold of you, you won't have a choice," the djinn said. "Death is the only option for you. It's the only way to save us all."

He flicked his wrist and his hand burst into flames. "We'll make it quick."

Fire. He had access to fire. Dad had told me enough about djinn to know that only the most powerful had access to elemental power on this plane, and even then it was short-lived access that drained them if used too frequently, which meant this djinn was no regular djinn.

Danger.

My sword was out of its sheath and at his throat in an instant. "I may not be able to kill you, but I can certainly mess up your pretty meat suit, so put the flames away."

"Meat suit? Is that what you think this is?" He blinked, and his eyes dulled to brown. "Don't. Don't kill me, please."

The tone of voice and the inflection were completely different. This was the human speaking, not the djinn. A human who was still very much alive and trapped. Fuck. It was one thing knowing the meat suits were human hosts, it was another being introduced to one and then killing it.

The djinn's eyes flared bright again. "It seems you have much to learn about djinn and our bonds. Our hosts don't die when we take over. They're alive, and we have the ability to free them. Are you willing to kill an innocent to save these Fangs?"

Dammit.

"Eva, just walk away," Jace said.

The doors of the van opened, and Logan and Ash stepped out. They were immediately surrounded by djinn intent on their execution.

Ash's jaw was tight, muscles bunched, ready to fight, but they were holding off. Holding off because of me. Holding off because the djinn were wearing innocent humans, and fighting them meant killing the hosts, it meant killing the humans. But if we didn't fight, we'd die, and the cure, which was in our grasp, would be lost. I could walk away, I should, but my chance of getting to the cure would be drastically diminished without the Fangs. Aside from which, despite the shit that had gone down between Logan, Jace, and me, the bastards had grown on me.

The situation was clear. This was a case of a handful of lives to save the many.

I locked gazes with Ash. "This is bigger than us. I need you guys. No matter what it takes."

A serene calm settled over his face and then his hands whipped out to grab the nearest djinn's head. There was a crack, and the djinn dropped to the ground. Black smoke rose out of the dead body and hovered in the air above it. Glowing eyes glared accusingly at Ash, and then all hell broke loose. Weapons whizzed through the air and bones cracked.

My sword hand faltered, and the leader made a lunge for me with his huge paw. I ducked to avoid his grasp, spinning around him to bring my sword back up but pulling back just in time to avoid decapitating him.

The edge of my steel lay snug against his throat once more. "Call off your djinn. Now."

But there was no need for him to say anything; his posse had backed off as soon as the metal had touched his skin again. They lowered their weapons, their fiery eyes fixed on me, on the blade kissing their leader's throat.

"I overestimated your humanity." The leader's

tone was bitter. "You'd kill innocents to save Fangs, Fangs that will probably be recruited by the Vladul and be used to enslave us all. While the rest of us work to counter the threat, you're acting to assist it."

Assist? He had no fucking clue. How dare he? "I'd kill a handful of innocents without a thought if it meant saving thousands more." The words were out before I could stop them. "Fuck."

He'd gone very still. "What do you mean? What are you talking about?"

"Eva …" Jace warned.

This was a fucked-up mess, and my gut told me that revealing the existence of the cure was the only way out of it. They were obviously against the Vladul and everything they stood for. The cure was the best way to take away the Vladul's leverage, and maybe if the djinn knew of its existence it would change things.

"There's a cure to the virus, and I'm on my way to get it." The words were out.

"You're lying." There was doubt in his statement, in his deep, gravelly voice.

"No. I'm not."

He was silent for a long beat. "No. You're not. You actually believe there is a cure."

"I know there is. And the Fangs are my security escort to get it. You kill them, you kill any chance of us getting the cure."

"If there is a cure, you don't need them to escort you. We'll take you to it ourselves."

"You could, but they're much prettier, and I like my eye-candy."

He let out a surprised snort. "There's a cure ... Well, I'll be damned."

"There is."

"Then that changes everything." Around us the djinn relaxed, muscles unknotting and eyes dimming. "You're free to go, but on two conditions."

"Funny how you get to make demands with a blade at your throat."

He laughed. "You won't kill me. You're smarter than that."

He was right. I lowered the sword. "Speak."

"We get to keep the van and any tech inside."

Ash nodded.

"Fine."

He smiled. "And one of my men goes with you."

"Like fuck," Logan said.

"We have a stake in this too. We all do, and djinn protection will come in useful on your journey."

"Eva, this is bullshit," Logan said.

"Is it?" Jace replied.

Ignoring them both, I focused on the djinn. "I agree to your terms, but I have a condition of my own."

He arched a brow.

"The djinn that comes with us won't be one of your men, it will be you."

The djinn around us broke out in protests, but the leader merely smiled. "I see you were raised by a tactician."

I returned his smirk. He had no idea. Having the leader in our grasp would keep the djinn in line. They were less likely to try something, like attacking us on our journey, if their leader was surrounded by Fangs. Maybe a regular djinn was disposable, but from their reaction to the blade at his throat, their leader wasn't. My instincts told me that the djinn genuinely wanted to help, but prudence stated that we keep some leverage.

"Well?" I arched a brow.

The djinn smiled. "Very well, you have a deal."

Chapter Four

What? What was this? Where was I? The world was a blur of bright light and sounds and smells. What had happened? Flashes of memory filtered through my mind. The Vladul female smirking, the dark-clothed Vladul entering the room, and the dart flying at me followed by a sharp sting in my neck. They'd knocked me out, drugged me. Urgh, no wonder my mouth tasted like ass.

I had to get up. I had to get out, but my body was immobile. Panic bloomed in my chest and surged up my throat.

No. Calm down and assess. Eva's voice cut through my panic. Thank God she was still with me.

Blinking several times brought the world into focus. I was upright in a glass tube of some sort in a lab, at least that's what it looked like with all the science-type equipment and clean white lines.

Test the bonds.

Right. Wrists and ankles, thighs and torso and, shit, neck. They weren't taking any chances. The panic was back, but I grit my teeth to stem it. A face appeared before me—the Vladul bitch.

"Heart rate is elevated," she said. "Scared?"

My first attempt at speech was a series of dry clicks. I worked my throat to moisten my mouth and tried again. "What are you doing to me?"

She smiled with one half of her mouth. "I'm going to turn you into a weapon, human. You'll be the Vladul's instrument of death."

"What are you talking about?"

Her lips remained frozen in a smug smirk.

An icy sensation flooded me. "What are you going to do to me?"

"Deana, we need to talk." A male figure appeared behind the female Vladul. "I saw something out there."

Deana turned away from me, dismissing me, her potential creation. "Elias, how good of you to finally come and see me."

The Vladul male's violet gaze flicked to me for a brief moment. "Sarcasm is beneath you, Deana."

"Once upon a time, it was you that was beneath

me." Her tone was suggestive and a far cry from her cruel, clinical demeanor.

Elias's smile was dry. "It was never me you wanted. It was my status you craved. Malcolm's right-hand man you wanted."

"Have you come here to reopen old wounds?" There was a pout to her tone, a coquettish lilt.

"No. I need your help."

"Really? And why should I do anything to help you?"

"Because this could benefit you too."

"I'm listening ..."

"When we raided the Feral roost, we were attacked by three uninfected Fangs. They had a human female with them, and she had a key around her neck. A key with the Genesis symbol on it." He arched a brow in prompt.

A girl with a key around her neck? Oh, God, he was talking about Eva.

Deana had gone very still. "Are you saying ..."

"It's exactly what I'm saying."

"It can't be."

"It has to be. The Genesis Foundation has only one master key, and Malcolm has it. But it looks like this girl may have another."

"And if we can get hold of it ..." Deana's voice was laced with excitement.

"Yes. We can finally wrest control of this place from him."

He wanted to go after Eva. Oh, God. I needed to get out of here. I needed to warn her. Damn these bonds. Damn getting captured. Fuck. Trapped. There was no getting out of here. Not until Deana was done with me.

Deana stepped up to Elias and tilted her head to look up into his face. "Go after the human and get the key. I'll cover for you. I'll put you on my security rotation." Her hand came up to cup the side of his face. "Elias, get that key, and we can rule side by side once more, as it was truly meant to be."

His cruel lips curled in a satisfied smile. "And Malcolm will finally taste true fear."

"Yes." The word was a sibilant hiss.

The male's gaze flicked to me. "And what is this you're playing with?"

She shrugged. "Just a little project for Malcolm."

Elias's eyes narrowed. "Now, now, Deana, do share."

"Bring back the key, and you'll unlock all my secrets," she said.

He gripped her shoulders. "Deana …"

She huffed. "It's a weapon, all right. And that's all I'm at liberty to say right now." She leaned into him, her lips inches from his. "But bring me the key and it's your weapon."

"Our weapon," he said. "How long until it's deployed?"

She puffed out her cheeks. "A week, at the most."

"Better if you hold off. We don't want Malcolm having control of it, do we?"

She arched a brow. "It hardly matters when the result will be the same whoever wields it."

His smile was slow to burn. "Oh, it matters, Deana. Especially if you want us to be remembered as the ones holding the reins."

She ran a finger down his chest. "I missed this, Elias. I'm glad you're back."

"Yes. So am I."

He stepped away from her touch, turned on his heel, and strode from the room. Her shoulders sagged briefly, but she pushed them back and clipped over to me.

"So, where were we? Oh, yes. We were about to begin your transformation." She reached up to press something to my left, something I couldn't turn my head to see, and then a hiss filled the glass chamber I was trapped in. "I warn you, it will be slow, and it will be painful."

What was that? Gas? No. I felt fine, what was

she doing? Something tickled my toes, cool and wet and ... Oh, shit. There was no doubt what that was.

I stared right into her eyes and clenched my jaw, defiant. "Fuck you, Deana. Fuck you."

The chamber filled with water.

Chapter Five

The djinn leader's fiery gaze had dimmed to a smooth gold now, like Noah's, but deeper, with flecks of silver that radiated outward from his pupils. This close, his huge frame dwarfed mine, and a steady heat radiated off his body to brush my skin. There was no way a human could be that big. This was djinn form given carbon substance by the bond he'd formed with a human.

"I'm Eva." I held out my hand, and he shook it.

The rasp of his palm sent a tingling sensation up my arm, and I pulled back quickly.

"My name is Sage," he said.

Not his true name, this would be a pseudonym, because djinn never gave out their birth names. To know a djinn's name gave you power over them; it was where the whole genie in a bottle metaphor had come from. Knowing a djinn's true name allowed you to summon them and force them to do your bidding, although I couldn't imagine Sage bowing to anyone. The creature was pure power trapped in material form.

Behind us, the other djinn were busy raiding the van. Ash stood to my right clutching two of our backpacks stocked with provisions for our journey. No tech inside, so they were ours per the deal I'd struck. Jace pressed a hand to his lips and then touched his bike in farewell before walking over to join us, while Logan hovered by the van, his eyes on the djinn who were combing through it.

A djinn jumped out of the van holding our radio.

"No." Logan made a grab for it. "Not that. We need that."

Sage frowned. "We had a deal."

Shit. I should have added that we get to keep the radio. We needed to stay in contact with Noah. But djinn were notoriously stubborn, and renegotiation was not an option.

Logan turned to look at Sage, his lip curl a warning he was about to unleash some choice curses. The Fang had a foul mouth, and the djinn had fiery hands. Not a great combination.

"Logan, back off." I stepped in front of Sage and then regretted the move. It looked like I was shielding him, which was ridiculous.

Logan's jaw tensed.

I walked over to the van and smiled up at the djinn who was holding the radio. "May I please make one more call before you take it? Just to let our friend know what's happened so he doesn't worry?"

The djinn looked over my head at Sage, who must have given the okay, because he handed me the radio.

Beside me Logan was a mass of tension. He didn't like this situation. He wasn't happy with the deal we'd made, and no doubt I'd hear all about it at some point, but fuck him, it had been the only option.

"Noah, you there? Over." Static followed. "Noah, hello. Over."

"Eva? Is everything okay? Over." Noah sounded out of breath, like he'd run to get to the radio.

"Yeah, we're okay, but we won't be able to call in for a while. We had an encounter with some djinn, but we're fine." I filled him in briefly on the deal. "So we won't be able to get in touch. Over."

There was a lengthy silence. "Is the djinn's name Sage? Over."

"Yeah. Do you know him? Over."

"Hand him the radio. Over."

I walked over to Sage and held out the radio. He took it with a frown. "Hello. Over."

"Sage, you bastard. How in the hell are you? Over."

"Noah? Is that really you? Over."

"The one and only. Over."

Sage's face had lit up. He ran a hand over his shaved head as his gaze went from Ash to Logan to Jace. "I see it now. I see these are your boys. They were so tiny when we met. Over."

"They were. It's been too long. Listen, Sage, they're headed somewhere very important. If I'd known where you were, I'd have asked them to swing your way, but I guess fate has done what I couldn't. Take care of them for me. Over."

Sage pressed his lips together, his attention on me. "You can count on it. Over."

"Godspeed, my friend. Over and out."

Sage stared at the radio for several beats, and then he handed it to me. "Keep it."

"Sage? What are you doing?" one of the djinn by the van asked.

"These are Noah's boys, and I owe him a debt. Take the vehicles, but they can keep the radio." He looked down at me. "Come with me. Our camp isn't far from here, and I want to show you something."

I looked up at the sky. The sun was high. "We need to be at our next stop before dark."

"An hour is all it will take," Sage said.

"We need to get moving," Logan insisted.

"Jace? Ash?"

I'd agreed on the deal without consulting them, acting on instinct, on the fact that I'd been calling the shots for a while now, so it was only fair to get a consensus on this.

Ash signed.

"We have time," Jace translated.

Logan threw up his hands. "Of course we do."

I smiled up at Sage. "In that case. Sure."

IT WAS a fifteen-minute trek with Sage leading the way through the abandoned remains of a town square, past derelict stores and a dry, cracked fountain, over cobbles overgrown with weeds, and onto a dirt track leading into a brief woodland filled with twittering birds.

The sound was sweet and unexpected. Even Logan stopped to listen for a moment. How long since I'd heard that sound? The compound had been the last place, our enclosed garden where we'd had birds and even the odd squirrel. Out here in the wide world, the sounds of nature were silent, interrupted only by the growl of Claws or the howl of Fangs, so this was an auditory treat.

"How much farther?" Jace asked.

"We're here," Sage said.

We stepped out of the woodland into a meadow dappled with white blooms and heavy with the scent of honeysuckle. In the distance were several colorful tents, and to the left of the tents was a long, squat building with smoke pluming out of the chimney. The air around the whole scene was a shimmering blue haze.

"What is it? What is that?" I pointed at the sky.

"A ward," Sage said. His long legs ate up the distance between us and the settlement. "This is our home. It's our base of operations."

"Operations?" Sounded official.

We were almost at the shimmer. It rose up to meet us, and then it was passing over my skin with a tingling sensation as I stepped through. Laughter and music greeted us, the sound of a baby crying, the aroma of roasting meat and the clang of metal on metal. So much sensory information in such a short space of time. It was overload, and it was glorious.

Humans milled about, smiling, happy, and at the sight of Sage several children came running up to us.

"Sage, Sage! What did you bring us today?"

He laughed and swung two of the younger boys up into his arms. "A big van for you to play in."

"Can I drive it?" one of the boys asked.

"I'll tell you what? As soon as your legs are long enough, I'll teach you." He set them down, and they ran off toward a bright yellow tent.

A golden-haired woman stepped out to greet them; she looked up and raised a hand in greeting to Sage. Her curious gaze fell to us, and she pressed her lips together and retreated into the tent.

As we made our way toward the huge building that looked like it had once been a barn, several other humans greeted Sage, mainly young human females with eyelashes that seemed to flutter too much and hands that seemed to touch a little more than necessary. The djinn was certainly popular with the ladies, and for a moment, I saw him the way they did. A beast of a man, with a grin that made mouths ache to smile and eyes that teased the soul. Yes, he was an attractive, compelling creature. And he could burn me to a crisp with a touch of his hand.

The doors to the barn were open wide, and the sound of machinery emanated from within.

"You live with the humans." Logan sounded stunned. "They ... like you."

"We saved them," Sage said. "We're a family here, and we take care of each other."

"Your hosts are voluntary, aren't they?" Jace said.

41

Sage smiled. "There is no other way to take a host. Not if you want it to retain its sanity."

"Not all djinn care about their human hosts' sanity," Logan said.

"No. Not all djinn do."

I hadn't even known that djinn could take human hosts until today, so this was all news to me. We were almost at the barn doors when a woman intercepted us.

"Sage, where are the others? Where's Henry? Juno returned a few minutes ago. He returned without Henry."

Sage's gaze flicked to Ash and then he sighed. "I'm sorry, Lia, there was an accident. Henry is dead." His words were simple and direct, but his tone was loaded with compassion.

Beside me, Ash stiffened. Henry must have been the host he'd killed. Killed on my say-so. I reached out and gave his hand a brief squeeze.

The woman shook her head. "No. No, he can't be. You said ... You said once this was over, I'd get him back."

"And that was our intention," Sage said. "Henry was a brave man. He offered himself to the cause, and he died in the pursuit of our freedom."

She rolled her lips into her mouth, her eyes brimming with tears.

Sage's hand swallowed her shoulder in a gesture

42

of comfort. "The others are bringing his body back. He will be given a warrior's burial."

Tears slipped down her cheeks, but she dashed them away with the back of her hand and lifted her chin. "I'll tell the others." She walked back toward the tents.

Sage blew out a breath.

This was our fault. "I'm sorry."

"No. You weren't to know. These things happen. Mortal life is fleeting and, consequently, more precious, but all our hosts knew the risks. They accepted willingly because our goal is worth the sacrifice."

He led us into the barn, where the hum of voices and the *buzz* and *whirr* of machinery filled the air. Several vehicles were parked to the right—a patchwork of various machines with huge tractor wheels and customized armor. Several had wicked-looking pikes jutting out all over the body work, and one had a huge machine gun on top of it. On the wall to the left were weapons—guns, knives, and grenade launchers. You name it, they had it.

"What is this?" Jace asked.

"This," Sage said, "is our arsenal." He walked ahead and then turned to face us. "This is how we're going to take down the Genesis Foundation."

Chapter Six

An armory ... The djinn had a fucking armory. How long had it taken for them to put this together?

Sage's gaze was hot on the side of my face. "You like?"

Forcing my gaze away from the weapons, I glanced up at him. "It's beautiful."

His broad face split into a huge grin. "I thought you might appreciate it."

"You did?"

He frowned and stared searchingly into my face. "In our realm, magic is power, but here, in this dimension, knowledge is power—the knowledge that leads to science, the science that creates weapons. You have a thirst for power inside you. A thirst for knowledge."

"Yes, I do, but how in the world could you know that? Djinn mojo?"

"No. I recognize a kindred spirit when I see one," he said.

Kindred spirit? "We're nothing alike."

His smile was cryptic. Djinn and their need to be mysterious. I didn't have time for guessing games and cryptic sentences. If he had something to say, he'd have to just come out and say it.

Ash was examining the nearest tank, his large hands running over the armored plating as if testing its validity. He turned to Logan, his hands moving fast. I'd gotten used to reading him, and the slight twitch of his left brow told me he was asking something, not making a statement.

"You're planning to storm Genesis, aren't you?" Logan asked on behalf of Ash. There was no mistaking the skepticism in his voice.

Sage's eyes narrowed. "You have a problem with that?" He addressed Ash, who simply shrugged.

But Logan wasn't so blasé. "We don't have a problem, but you might. You have the weapons and the vehicles, but you don't have the manpower. You have what? Ten, maybe eleven djinn?"

Sage lifted his chin. "The humans allied with us will fight."

Logan arched a brow. "You're serious?" He

shook his head. "The Vladul will *literally* eat the humans alive."

"The humans are aware of the risk. They realize what is at stake," Sage said.

In other words, they were willing to act as cannon fodder. But why were the djinn making such an effort to attack the Genesis Foundation? What was it that they planned to achieve? It made no sense ... They'd get in, but then what? The Vladul had the numbers. They'd fight back, and the djinn and their meager human posse would fall. Unless ... Unless the djinn did have an army ...

Comprehension bloomed in my chest. "The Vladul have your people, don't they?"

Sage's amber eyes flared to life like dying embers given a fresh breath of air. "Yes. Your deduction skills are impressive."

"Once you're in, you'll free them, and they'll take human hosts, humans you'll be taking in with you. You'll have your army." How was that for deduction?

"That's the plan." Sage crossed his arms.

It was a good plan. A really good plan. Once we had the cure, once we'd deployed it, I could go with them and get Tobias out. This was fate, it had to be.

"When do you plan to act?" Jace asked.

"We're almost ready," Sage said. "But a cure trumps our plan. The cure must come first."

Yes. It had to come first. It was the only reason I was here and not trying to break into the Genesis Foundation right now. "If we get the cure, the Vladul's days will be numbered. Once the Feral and the Fangs are restored, there'll be more of us than them. When that happens, I'm coming with you. I'm storming their stronghold."

Sage nodded, a smile hovering on his lips. "And you will be welcome."

"Unless the cure is more of a vaccine to protect the uninfected," Jace pointed out. "We won't know if it can actually *cure* the Feral until we have more information."

He wasn't being negative, just pointing out the facts, but it grated anyway, and the cold look I gave him had him ducking his head and averting his gaze. Shit, I needed to rein in the animosity with him. What had happened had been a one-off. Jace had slipped up and almost allowed his brother to drain me. His apology had been sincere. I needed to cut him a break. Jace glanced my way again, and I shot him a smile, but it sat stiff and unnatural on my face.

"We should get going," Logan said. "We have only a few hours of sunlight left. We need to get to the bunker."

Sage's brows shot up. "A bunker? As in government-issue?"

"Yes, and before you ask, you can have any

useful tech once we're done with the place." I headed for the exit. "Sun's wasting, guys, let's move out."

THE BUNKER ENTRANCE was buried beneath weeds and thorns and located under a cement bridge on the bank of a rushing river. Hydraulic power. The other bunkers would be the same, no doubt, built beside rivers and lakes to harness the water's power for their generators. Clever.

The codes that Noah had given us were in no particular order, and it was the third one down that opened the thick metal hatch with an ominous hiss. Stale air rushed out to greet us.

Yeah, this bunker hadn't been used in a long while, if ever.

Ash placed a hand on my shoulder and gave it a gentle squeeze. It was his cue for me to step back and allow him to go first. I obliged, and he slipped past me and dropped down into the hatch. Boots clanged on metal as he descended the ladder, and then there was silence.

"Let me." Logan went next, dropping into darkness.

"All good?" Jace called down.

A soft red light bloomed in the dark.

"Clear." Logan's voice echoed off the metal walls.

I lowered myself into the hatch and began to climb. Red bulbs were set in the wall periodically, lighting the way. This bunker was deeper than the one Noah and the guys had commandeered, although the room I landed in was roughly the same size as the one at our bunker.

Our bunker? Getting cozy was not a good idea.

Logan stood by the door leading into the main part of the structure, but Ash was nowhere to be seen.

I glanced past him. "Where's Ash?"

"He's inside," Logan said. "He put the power on, and he's doing a sweep."

Jace landed lightly behind me, followed by Sage. The djinn's huge frame ate up what was left of the space, leaving it suddenly claustrophobic and close.

"We could have stayed at my base," he said. "The wards would have kept us safe."

"We could have, but then we'd have had a longer journey tomorrow. This works best. Also you get to scope out the tech and set what you want aside for the return journey." I wiggled my brows at him.

Sage's surprised chuckle was low and sexy.

Logan rolled his eyes. "If you've finished flirting

with Mr. Smokeless Fire, then maybe you'd like to go through?" He swept an arm out toward the entrance.

What? "I wasn't flirting. I don't flirt."

Jace cleared his throat. "Maybe we should just go through?"

Logan dismissed me with a flick of his lashes and headed into the bunker. Jace followed quickly, as if eager to get away from me.

"After you," Sage said, with more than a hint of amusement in his tone.

His scent was electric, like the beginning of a storm. It had the hairs on my nape quivering and made me want to lean back into him. Instead, I stepped away and through the door. Away from the tingle his presence sent down my spine.

A CONTROL ROOM, six cabins, a lounge, a kitchen, and a shower room with two toilets. It was cozy and functional, and damn, was I hungry.

Sage and I sat at the table, scoffing our faces. We were the only ones needing actual food for sustenance, so we'd gravitated to the kitchen together. The place was stocked well, dried goods and tinned goods and long-life milk that had unfortunately gone off, but there was powdered milk too and we'd made hot chocolate for after.

Sage was on his fifth can of tinned food, and I was on my third. The cans were papered in white with the names of the food neatly printed on. This was government-issue food, and there was no "best before" date printed anywhere on the tin. I'd gone for ravioli, garden peas, and was rounding off with some pineapple chunks. Sage had eaten five tins of beans for the protein value. Everything tasted slightly metallic, but it was food and it was good.

The djinn sat back and licked his lips. "Did you know you make these little cute snuffly sounds when you eat?"

A chunk of pineapple got lodged in my throat for a second. Had I heard him right?

His gaze dropped to my lips, dimming then flaring bright. "It's ... distracting."

Okay, this was flirting, and the frisson of pleasure it sent through me was overshadowed by annoyance.

I set down my fork and can. "Don't."

"Don't?" His smile was knowing.

I met his gaze with a level one of my own. "I don't do flirting, Sage. It's a waste of energy and time."

He canted his head, his fiery eyes narrowing to slits. "Is it?" He tapped an index finger on the table.

"I think it lightens the mood. It's fun and it can make you feel good. But I get you like to keep that side of you under lock and key." He picked up his can of food. "I can understand that you're a warrior, and warriors know how to compartmentalize."

Is that what I did? Put my emotions in neat boxes? Tobias ... Yes. I'd done that with Tobias and lost the chance to tell him how I felt. I picked up the penknife I'd found in one of the drawers and began to fiddle with it.

"Your problem is the compartment marked 'levity' is permanently sealed," he added.

Fire licked at the base of my throat. "I can have fun, Sage. But right now, while we chase a cure that could save the world, isn't the time to do it."

"And it wasn't the time before either, was it? When would the best time be? When the world ends?"

The fire died. "It won't end. We'll make sure of it."

"While having zero fun?" His grin was wicked and roguish.

Despite my best efforts, a smile teased my lips.

He ducked his head. "Aha, she smiles."

"Why do you care?"

Confusion painted his features and then his mouth turned down. "Honestly, I'm not sure."

Our gazes locked, and an indecipherable awareness leapt between us. I was first to drop my gaze.

"You best eat up." Sage's gravelly voice was delicious friction to my senses. "Your Fangs are
hungry."

Well *poof* went the delicious friction. Instead, my
stomach tightened in apprehension. Yes, the Fangs
were waiting for me. Waiting until I'd fueled up, so
they could feed off me. The thought sent a shudder
rippling through me.

Sage's jaw hardened. "You're afraid." He sat
forward. "Have they hurt you? They may be Noah's
boys, but they're still Fangs, and if they've hurt
you, then—"

I held up a hand to stall his words. "I'm fine. I
made a deal, and I intend to honor it."

He snorted. "A very djinn thing to say."

I smiled at him. "Is it?"

He nodded slowly. "Yes. We are slaves to honor,
but we know how to give our word and yet keep
hold of it at the same time." His smile was conspiratorial. "I can teach you, if you like?"

Why did it seem like he was offering to undress
me? "I'm good. Thanks."

He spooned some more food into his mouth.

But my curiosity about him, about the djinn as a
race had been piqued. "Is that where the whole *be
careful what you wish for* warning comes from?"

He swept his tongue across his bottom lip. "We don't grant wishes, but we do like to play with words. And yes, you must always be wary when making a deal with a djinn."

"Well, my deal doesn't really have any wiggle room. They helped me try and save my friends, and in return I agreed to be their walking blood bag until they found a replacement."

His brows shot up. "And did you save your friends?"

"No. One died, and the other ... The other was taken by the Vladul." I met his gaze. "But I'm going to get him back."

"Is that why you wish to come with us when we attack the Foundation?"

"Yes. I can't let him languish there."

"You love him," he said bluntly.

My pulse skipped. "He's my best friend."

"That too. But you love him as well."

My cheeks grew warm. "And how would you know?"

He shrugged. "Your heart beat faster when you were talking about him, and your pupils dilated a fraction. Aside from that, I can taste it in your words."

I let out a snort. "*Taste* that I'm in love with my best friend?"

That same conspiratorial smile. "There are many

things that djinn see that humans and other creatures can't. Voices and music have distinct shapes
and colors that change and shift depending on the
speaker's emotions and who they are speaking to."

He could see my words? "And what else have
you learned?"

He dropped his gaze almost coquettishly. "If I
told you all your secrets it would ruin your journey
of self-discovery."

"Fuck self-discovery. I'm all about the information, right here and right now."

"I know you are. It's your hunger. But sometimes information, emotions, and relationships need
to be left to stew before they can fully mature." He
looked up, his lips toying with a smile. "I *can* tell you
that you're attracted to me, though."

"Am I? I hadn't noticed." My tone was flippant.

Thank goodness for my poker face. I'd been
blocking my physical reaction to him. Ignoring how
every time his eyes flared, something inside me
tightened in anticipation of something I didn't
understand, or how every time he got close enough
for his body heat to brush against my skin, a delicious shiver ran up and down my spine. It had to
have been because of the otherworldly magic that
coursed through his veins.

Now was the time to say something to deny the
attraction, but the words stuck in my throat.

Instead, I deliberately scooped some pineapple into my mouth and chewed it slowly. His gaze dropped to my lips and lingered for a moment.

He finally leaned back and grinned, flashing his perfect white teeth. "Don't worry. It's reciprocated."

Oh, fuck. What did I say to that?

Ash appeared in the doorway, breaking the tension. His attention fell to the empty cans and then rose up to skim my throat. My breath caught, because yes, he was here for the power that flowed through my veins.

"I'm ready." With a sigh, I pushed back my seat and slid the penknife into my pocket. "Let's get this done."

Sage's expression was suddenly serious, making me wonder what color my words were now?

Chapter Seven

A sh led me down the corridor to the control room. We'd decided on the public place to do this. Decided that everyone would be present, so no one lost their head. They'd feed enough to take the edge off their hunger and no more. There would be no repeat of the Logan incident. There would be no oops, I almost drained you.

Logan and Jace were leaning up against the long desk that sat under a bank of blank monitors. They were both dressed in the regulation black combat trousers and shirts that seemed to come as standard with these bunkers, but Logan's hair was damp and swept off his forehead and his designer stubble had been neatened up. He'd obviously showered. He'd rolled up his sleeves to expose his powerful forearms, which were crossed over his

57

chest almost defensively, as if it were me that was coming to take something from him, not the other way around. Even his expression was accusing. God, he was infuriating.

Jace's smile was fleeting, almost nervous, and he looked like he'd spent ages raking his hand through his dark hair.

Sage trailed into the room behind us and leaned against the doorframe. His massive body blocked the exit, and his arms were folded loosely across his chest. Strange that between him and Ash, the task at hand didn't seem so daunting.

Ash locked gazes with Sage and the djinn's eyes dimmed a little. It was almost as if they were communicating, but that was ridiculous, right? Okay, focus and breathe. This would be over quickly. It was clinical, and it was … man, who was I kidding. I was lunch.

Ash pulled me against his chest.

"And why do you get to go first?" Logan's voice was thicker. A sign of his hunger?

Dammit, we should have done this before we'd left the main bunker, but after Jace had extracted enough blood to keep Noah going while we were gone, I'd been pretty woozy. The Fangs had agreed to wait for our first stop.

And here it was.

My hands grasped at Ash's waist, and his grip

on me tightened. He cupped the base of my skull, fingers sliding through my hair as he tilted my head to the side. My nose brushed his chest as he cradled me.

"I think he wants us to drink while he holds her," Jace said to Logan.

Sage's snort was saturated with derision. "So, which one of you is it that can't be trusted?"

Jace's sigh was loaded with emotion.

"Really?" Sage said. "I'd have thought it was Logan."

"It is me," Logan said. "I'm the one she doesn't trust."

Was that regret tinging his tone?

Ash's lips brushed the top of my head, and then heat caressed my back.

"Don't worry," Logan said tightly. "I'll make it quick and painless."

"No." My tone came out sharper than intended. "Don't take the pain away."

The last thing I needed was to be moaning and tingling with endorphins while he took what he needed. The thought made my stomach ache.

Logan's chuckle was a raw thing. "Riiight ... Have it your way." His lips touched my skin. "You better brace yourself, Eva."

The puncture was quick, sharp, and deep, and my resulting gasp was just as sharp. Logan began to suck, and my artery burst into flame. My scream was sudden and involuntary, filling the room with the echo of my pain. But the fire was racing outward, spreading, burning brighter and brighter. No thought, no thought. Oh, God. No. No.

"Logan, dammit!" Jace's voice was a whiplash.

His lips left my neck for a brief second, taking the fire with them. "She asked for this." Anger, real and potent, coated those words.

Ash's chest vibrated against me. No more. Don't let him hurt me. The words were locked on my tongue, buried under the aftershocks of agony as I tried to pull free of Ash.

"Fine," Logan said.

His lips found my neck again. "No." The word was a weak plea.

Ash's fingers caressed my scalp, stilling me, reassuring me, and then ice froze the fire in its tracks, soothing and calming. Fire? What fire? Oh, God. Thank God. The ice simmered into a teasing, caressing heat. It was happening, the thing where my body revolted on my mind, where my nipples tightened and my abdomen contracted. This was a new kind of torment. Give me the fire instead.

No. "Stop. Don't."

My words were garbled, as if I'd been drugged, which I had because Logan had flooded me with incubus endorphins, and the thoughts, all the fucking thoughts going through my mind were naked and carnal and—

"Stop." My voice came out sure and strong this time.

The warmth of Logan's mouth on my skin retreated with a flick of his tongue. "Fuck …" He staggered away, taking his body heat with him. "Fucking hell." Something scraped across the floor. A chair?

"Shit, Logan. Sit." Jace's concern was evident in his tone, but my body was still floating, slowly coming back to earth. I hated that it wasn't mine to control, that they could have this effect on me against my will. That for those long seconds, my body hadn't been my own.

A sob caught in my throat as Jace took Logan's place. Oh, God. Again. I'd have to relinquish control again. Ash's body tensed.

"It's okay, Eva. I'll make it quick," Jace said softly. "I wish … I wish I didn't need this."

"No endorphins." I pushed the words out through gritted teeth.

"I'm sorry, I can't control that aspect like Logan can." He sounded genuinely apologetic. "It doesn't work that way with me."

Ash's fingers massaged the nape of my neck reassuringly. I lifted my chin to look up into his face. My gaze grazed his stubbled chin and caressed his lips before meeting his pale irises. My reflection stared back at me from his obsidian pupils — lips parted in a daze. I clamped my mouth shut and clenched my jaw.

Hated this. Fucking hated it.

"I'm going to touch you now," Jace said. His tone was lower, slightly breathless. It sent a tremor through me. "Close your eyes, Eva."

My eyelids fluttered closed and then his fingers came to rest lightly on the column of my neck in the valley that led to the slope of my shoulder. Okay, this wasn't so bad. His touch was light and non-invasive. Was he feeding? Was this it? I opened my mouth to ask just as my skin began to tingle. It was a slight buzz at first, just beneath the pads of his fingertips, unnerving but not uncomfortable.

Ash's arm around my waist flexed and a low rumble vibrated in his chest. A warning.

"I know." Jace's tone was tight, almost as if he was in pain. "Just a little more."

The buzz intensified, spreading across my skin and seeping into my veins, and then every nerve in my body came to life, fizzing and writhing and wrestling an unwanted moan from my lips. No. Not again. Fuck this. I bit down on my bottom lip hard enough to draw blood and not caring. Just no more moans. No more.

The sensual tremors passed through me, down

to the place that throbbed and ached with a need that was private and, right now, unwelcome. Ash's body tensed against me. His lips found the crown of my head, pressing against my scalp soothingly. The action diverted my attention to his mouth, to his body, to him.

Jace's fingers were gone, but my body was still rippling with sensation.

"Ash." His name was a soft exhalation on my lips.

And then his hand was tightening in my hair, enough to tilt my head up, enough to force me to look into his unfathomable eyes. *My turn*, they said, and then his mouth claimed mine. There was no holding back this time. No pulling away, because he needed this, and I ... I wanted it. The unease that had gripped me under Logan's and Jace's attentions melted away, and a new kind of heat unfurled in my belly. I pushed up on tiptoe and raked a hand through his hair, opening for him, claiming his tongue and tasting him as he was tasting me. He pulled back slightly, mouth parted, and his fangs slid out farther from his gums, reminding me what he was and what he needed. A spike of adrenaline shot through me, but instead of pulling me away from him, it drew me closer, flush up against his chest, so my breasts were pressed against his taut pectorals. Ash's fangs didn't repel me. Instead, my pulse throbbed, eager to submit beneath them.

"Take what you need." My words were a breathless whisper against his lips.

He pressed his forehead to mine and then ran the tip of his nose down the side of my face and into the curve of my neck, then back up until his mouth was settled over my artery. He laved the spot with his tongue, once, twice, and my body shuddered in response, and then he slid into me, smooth and practiced, and fuck, the world was a rainbow of sensation. Glitter and disco balls and every inch of my body was charged with energy and need and want, and yes, I wanted his mouth back on mine — coppery and sweet and intoxicating. Our tongues wrestled in a match that neither of us wanted to win because it was about tasting and submitting.

"Ahem!"

Ash broke the kiss, eyes bright beneath inky lashes on lids lowered to half-mast.

My heart. Oh, my heart …

His thumb ran across my bottom lip, light and yet possessive, and then he carefully set my feet back on the ground.

Logan slow clapped. "Well, well, well. Who'd have thought Ash had it in him."

"Shut up, Logan," Jace admonished.

I straightened my spine and turned to face them.

Logan was wearing his habitual cocky expression while Jace just looked plain uncomfortable. But Sage was looking from Ash to me with a narrow-eyed intensity.

I cleared my throat. "Now that everyone has ... eaten, we should get some rest. We have a long day ahead of us tomorrow."

I strode from the room, neck hot and scalp prickling. Shit. I'd just made out with a Fang in full view of an unwilling audience, and the only thought going through my head was, when could I do it again?

SLEEP WAS PROVING to be elusive and my cabin felt claustrophobic. Maybe a walk would help. The corridors were empty beneath a blanket of silence as I wandered toward the small lounge area. Orange leather sofas and a bright green rug greeted me, as if whoever had decorated the dismal gray space had been desperate to brighten it at all costs, but honestly the combination was sickly and invasive on the senses.

I parked myself on the sofa, leaned back, and closed my eyes as exhaustion washed over me. My butt was still numb from the long van ride, my body exhausted from the adrenaline of meeting the djinn, and my emotions awry from being fed on by Logan and Jace. Ash ... Ash was a different story. For some reason, my body craved his fangs, craved his proximity in a way I'd never experienced with anyone before. It was obvious what was happening. I was falling for the guy, but it was different from the way it had been with Tobias. With my best friend, the falling had been a gradual thing, born more of needing to protect him and keep him safe. He'd become my responsibility and then subsequently wormed his way into my heart. But with Ash, the connection had been there from the start, from the moment he'd first healed me.

The truth was that my cabin didn't feel claustrophobic, quite the opposite—it felt empty without Ash.

This was the last thing I needed. This craving, this distraction. With Tobias, I'd been able to turn it off, push it to the back of my mind and just get on with the task at hand. But then the responsibility of the key had been resting on my shoulders, and now there were several burly shoulders to carry that responsibility with me. It was as if something inside me was awakening. A new hunger, a new awareness, and I wasn't sure how much longer she'd be denied.

The sound of boot falls drifted through the open

lounge door, and Sage entered the room a moment later carrying two steaming mugs.

He didn't look surprised to see me. "I made some hot chocolate." He held out a mug.

He'd changed out of his vest and jeans into black combat trousers and a tight black T-shirt that strained across his chest becomingly. Becomingly? Where the hell had that come from?

I took the mug from him. "How did you know I'd be here?"

"Oh, Eva, I could track you to the ends of the earth."

His words were delivered in an echoing tone that sent a shudder up my spine.

"Huh?"

"Joking. Lucky guess." He lowered himself onto the sofa across from me.

Damn. For a moment, I'd believed him. "I see you found the stash of regulation wear."

He glanced down at himself. "The government seems to like black."

"It hides stains well. Although I'm surprised you were able to find anything that fit."

He leaned back in his seat, head tilted slightly to the side, rings winking in his earlobes. The mug clutched in his hand looked like a toy, barely a couple of sips for him.

"I can make them fit," he said.

"And how do you do that?"

His tongue peeked out to touch the corner of his mouth. "I make the carbon atoms in this body expand to fit my djinn form, and I can manipulate the fibers of clothing to fit my form."

"So, this *is* what you really look like?"

"Do you like what you see, Eva?"

Did I? I studied him, my mind seriously contemplating the question. His skin was tanned brown, stretched smooth over muscle and sinew, and his face was all broad planes and burning eyes. I didn't usually find guys with shaved heads attractive, but Sage was a different kind of animal.

My mouth was suddenly dry, and a scalding hot gulp of hot chocolate had me spluttering all over the place. Sage was out of his chair and patting me on the back in a blink.

"Shit, sorry." There was humor in his tone.

"No, you're not." I looked up at him. "You just wanted an excuse to touch me." The words surprised me, as did my teasing tone. I pressed my lips together. "I'm sorry. I don't know why I said that. Like I said earlier, I don't flirt."

"Or maybe you've just never had the freedom to." His huge hand was still on my back. "You know better than anyone else how short life can be. You've been fighting to survive for years, but what's the point in survival if you never actually live? You need to take your pleasures where you can find them."

I shifted so his hand fell away from my back. "It's a lovely concept. But it's not how I operate. It isn't how I was raised."

He stepped away with a slow blink. "Yes. I see that, but maybe it's time for a little re-education."

My stomach fluttered. His words spoke of emotional freedom, something I'd always kept on a tight leash because emotions clouded judgment and a slip in judgment could get you killed. But there was a cure, and soon my mission would be complete. My chest tightened. Who would I be without focus? Who would I be without a promise to keep and a world to save?

Not something that needed to be dwelled on right now.

I drained my mug and stood. "I should get some sleep."

Sage didn't protest. Instead he settled back into his chair with his beverage. "Sleep well, Eva, and think on my offer."

Offer? His offer of re-education? There was no doubt in my mind what that meant. His offer was purely carnal, and damn if it didn't send a frisson of speculation coursing through my veins.

I paused at the door. "Why me? There were lots of human females at your camp, and several of them looked more than interested in some *re-education*."

His smile was a slow burn. "Yes, there are, but none like you, Eva." He shot me a sidelong glance. "I know what I want, and it's been too long since I came face to face with it."

"Even though you think I'm in love with my best friend?"

He frowned slightly. "Is love finite? Are you saying your heart isn't big enough to love and be loved by more than one man?"

What was he saying? "When did *re-education* become love? Besides, relationships don't work that way."

His tongue teased the inside of his cheek. "Relationships can work any way you want, if you want them enough. Besides, in a world where there are more males than females, us males are going to have to learn to share." He sipped his drink. "Get some rest. You're going to need it."

I left him to his cryptic words and his tempting smile and headed out of the lounge. It was only when I was halfway down the corridor that I realized he hadn't responded fully to my question about love.

TWO MINUTES LATER, I found myself outside Ash's cabin staring at the door. My feet hadn't brought me here in error, I hadn't been daydreaming. I'd come here because I needed him. Ash, who drew me, captivated me, and made me feel safe. There'd be no sleep tonight without him. Coming here was admitting something, it was building something, but there would be no words, only the beat of his heart against my back when he rolled onto his side and pulled me against his chest, only the sound of his steady breath as I slipped into slumber.

Sage's words echoed in my mind, his spiel about time being short and his assertion that my heart was large enough to love more than one man. Maybe he was right, because despite the way I felt about Tobias, Ash was winding his way into my heart without uttering a word.

I pushed open the door and stepped into the room.

Ash was awake, propped up against the headboard, chest bare, book in hand. He looked up as I entered, then went back to reading. I kicked off my boots and then padded over to the bed. A T-shirt, *his* T-shirt, lay on the bed beside him. His attention was on his book, and so I yanked my top off and slipped his shirt on. It fell to mid-thigh. Last few times we'd slept together, I'd kept my slacks on, but that hadn't been the most comfortable night's sleep. Ash was focused on the page, but had his shoulders tightened? I slipped out of the slacks and climbed onto the bed beside him. The sheets were cool against my bare legs as I rolled onto my side and pulled my knees up.

A moment later, the bed jiggled and then the room was plunged into darkness. Ash's arm fell across my waist, and he gently pulled me back against his chest. My eyes fluttered closed as he rested his chin on the top of my head. He was curled around me, cocooning me in his heat, no need for a blanket. His hand lay on the bed by my abdomen, and I placed my palm on top of it, splayed my fingers, and then laced them with his. The hitch of his breath was the only indication he was affected by the contact.

Yes, this was starting something, and I wasn't one to start stuff I was unable to finish; it was why I'd held back with Tobias despite my feelings, but things were different now. There was hope, real hope, and maybe ... maybe it was possible to be selfish, just for once.

With a sigh, I closed my eyes and allowed his even breath to lull me to sleep.

YEARS OF LIGHT SLEEPING, of being on the run, had

trained me to wake at the drop of a hat, and so when something brushed the back of my neck my body responded by switching on to full alert in a second. Adrenaline flooded my body, readying it for action, and then my surroundings filtered in. Ash's cabin, his scent. My legs entwined with his, and his hand, warm and calloused, on my upper thigh.

His breath tickled the back of my neck, skimming over my skin, and that damn adrenaline, needing somewhere to go and something to do, had me pushing back into him.

He hardened against me and his low moan joined the skim of air at my nape. His hand on my thigh flexed, fingers digging into my flesh slightly.

Was he awake? God, this felt good. I pushed back again, this time rolling my hips against his crotch. His hand slipped up my thigh and under my shirt to skim the hem of my panties.

Heat and wetness bloomed, preparing me for his touch, a touch I needed and wanted. I covered his hand with mine, pulling it around to cup me. His breath hitched, and his heartbeat thrummed faster against my back. But then his body tensed around me. Shit. Had I misread this? Had he been asleep?

My neck heated, and I released his hand. "I'm sorry." My words were an embarrassed whisper. "I thought—"

I was flipped onto my back and then Ash

covered my body with his, settling between my thighs, his torso hovering over me, braced by powerful arms. His eyes gleamed in the gloom, tracking over my face as if absorbing every tiny detail.

He saw best in the dark, but what did he see when he looked at me? A woman eager to finally close her eyes and freefall? What was I seeing? A man teetering on the brink of relinquishing control. The knowledge sent a wicked thrill through me.

"Ash ..." I reached up to touch his cheek lightly with my fingertips.

His eyes fluttered closed briefly, and when he opened them there was a question glaring back at me.

I dragged my fingers across his lips, my body singing with need, and no, I didn't want to deny it any longer. "Yes. I want you."

His throat bobbed and then he lowered his body onto me inch by inch, pressing me into the mattress. Even with the fabric between us, the heat from his arousal set me on fire, forcing me to push into him, desperate to be closer.

He let out a low hiss, turning his face to the side as if in pain, but in the next instant my wrists were pinned above me and his mouth was on mine. He claimed me with tongue and lips and fang, hips rolling against me, rubbing and teasing until my gasps and whimpers of need were the only sounds that filled the room. His fangs grazed my neck, tongue laving across my sensitized flesh, but he pulled back, eyes squeezed shut in denial.

He didn't want to feed from me. But this was different. This would be a carnal feeding, a sexual act, and fuck, I wanted it. Chest heaving with a tumult of desire, I cupped his face.

"Take it. I want you to take it."

He opened his eyes and locked me in his sights, pupils so large his eyes were almost nothing but obsidian pools.

"I need you inside me, Ash. In every way."

He pressed a hard kiss to my mouth and then reached down and pulled up my shirt. I sat up, and he yanked it over my head, exposing me completely. He sat back on his haunches, taking me in, his bare chest moving rapidly with his excited breath. God, he was beautiful, all taut muscle, velvet skin, and abs.

He placed a huge hand on my chest, just over my breastbone, fingers splayed across my breasts, and then he pushed me down into the mattress, pinning me.

What? What was he doing?

He leaned down to press his mouth to my hip, trailing kisses inward toward my pubic bone. Oh, God. Oh, fuck. Tongue and the scrape of fang, and my mind was ready to shatter when he licked the inside of my thigh, moving up to my femoral artery. Was he? His tongue laved the spot. Yes. He was.

My hips bucked as his fangs slid into me, body arching as he began to feed, pouring ecstasy into me. My hands cupped the back of his head, torn between tearing him free and urging him to continue, because it was too much—too much sensation, firing up every synapse and heightening every inch of flesh, leaving me throbbing and aching and sobbing with a tangled web of conflicting emotions. And then his coppery mouth was on mine, tongues tangling in a kiss that almost stopped my heart.

Hands on my thighs, parting me, forcing my knees up as he positioned himself at my entrance.

"Please …"

He swallowed my plea and answered it by entering me. We rocked together for a long minute as my body adjusted to him, as I wrapped him in my heat and wetness. He moaned into my mouth as I flexed around him. Mine. This was mine. He pulled back to stare deep into my eyes, and then he began to move, and the world shattered into a million pieces.

THE SOUND of the shower running drifted out from the bathroom. Ash had left the door ajar, an invitation to join him, and damn, did I want to take him up on that. But we were about to step back into the real world, back to fighting for our lives. Back to the mission, and there was no place for romance outside. Best to rein it in. The bed lay rumpled and used before me, a witness to our passion.

There'd been barely any sleep. Just soft, lingering kisses; gentle, questing caresses; and a communication that transcended words. Ash had held me for hours as we'd inched toward dawn. He'd taken me again and again, claiming not just my body but also my heart. The bed held the shattered pieces of the wall that Ash had brought down.

I was no virgin. There'd been one guy three years ago—Justin, blond and blue-eyed. He and his parents had joined Dad, Tobias, and me for a couple of months. We'd lived in a vault at a bank then and things had happened. But it had been fumbling and awkward and painful, an experience I'd pushed to the back of my mind, but Ash had played my body with expert passion, and the part of me that I'd buried, the woman who longed for more than just survival, had awoken.

Here's to hoping she didn't get me killed.

Ash joined me by the bed. He cupped my shoulders with his large hands, hands that now knew my body intimately.

I looked up into his face. "This isn't just a casual thing for me."

He nodded.

"But you need to know that I love Tobias. I have for a while, which should mean that this ... what I feel for you shouldn't be possible, but it is, so ..." Sage's words filtered through my mind. I offered him half a smile. "I guess I have heart enough to want you both."

His grip on my shoulders tightened, and his silver eyes gleamed. He dropped a soft kiss on my forehead and then pressed his nose to my crown and inhaled me.

My eyes fluttered closed for a moment as I reveled in his acceptance of what I'd said, and then he took my hand in his and led me from the room.

I guess it was time to get down to business.

JACE, Logan, and Sage greeted us in the control room. They had a map spread out on a table and were plotting the next leg of our journey. Black combat clothes and kick-the-shit-out-of-you boots made up the ensemble. They looked professional and dangerous, and with their weapons laid on the counter behind them, they looked ready to take on whatever.

"I'm telling you that route will take us through the Wilds," Sage said.

Jace pouted, his blue eyes narrowed as he studied the map. "If we skirt it, we won't make it to the shack before sundown."

"Then we go through it," Logan said. "Just a quarter of a mile in and we shave three hours off our journey. It's a no-brainer."

"It isn't safe," Sage said.

"Scared?" Logan taunted the djinn.

Sage looked away, not taking the bait.

Jace moved back to make room as I stepped up to the table to study the map, but Logan stood his ground. His arm brushed mine, and the muscles in his biceps tensed. Great, he was happy to have physical contact when he was chowing down on me, but a casual brush and he was stiff as a board.

Jace had plotted our route neatly in red ink, and a blue shaded area marked the Wilds, courtesy of Sage, no doubt. We had three hundred miles to go, which would take around five days on foot with appropriate rest breaks. It was clear that if we took our original route, we wouldn't make it to our first overnight rest stop before nightfall. A shortcut through the Wilds would shave sixty miles off our journey and get us to our first rest stop before sundown—a place Noah had called The Shack. Noah and the guys had identified safe spots to hole up for the night based on their travels. The Shack was a store in an abandoned service station that they'd used on several occasions. It was off one of the main roads we'd need to follow to get to Kirkstone Pass; after that we were headed to Forest Noir to take refuge with a pack of Claws that Noah had befriended a few years ago.

I stepped back. "We need to do whatever it takes to avoid being stranded outside after dark. Pack some food and supplies and let's move out."

"Who died and left you in charge?" Logan asked.

"The same person that gave you your shitty attitude."

I stalked out of the room, intent on getting to the kitchen and grabbing some tins, but a hand snagged my elbow and yanked me in the opposite direction and into a small storage cupboard.

Logan's familiar vanilla scent wrapped around me, but before I could react he'd shoved me up against the wall and pressed his palms to the brick on either side of me.

His chocolate brown eyes bore into mine. "You reek of Ash. He's all over you. You fucked him, didn't you?"

My neck heated, but not with shame, with anger. "Who I fuck is none of your business."

"It is when it's Ash. He's not like me or Noah or Jace. You want to scratch an itch then you can come to one of us. We'll take it in turns to service you. But keep your arse out of Ash's bed. He feels things intensely. He connects, and he gives too much of a damn." He pushed away from the wall and turned his back on me, running a hand over his head. "I knew you were trouble the moment I saw him cradling you in his arms when we picked him up outside Haven, and then when he attacked me over you … Nah, I'm not letting you use him to control us."

Wait, what? He thought I was playing Ash? "I'm not using Ash. I have genuine feelings for him, and FYI, I don't usually fuck Fangs. In fact, I don't usually fuck, full stop."

He gave me an incredulous look over his shoulder. "Yeah? And what about Tobias? You're telling me you two haven't fucked."

Were we really having this conversation? I lifted my chin. "That's exactly what I'm saying."

"But you're in love with him."

Fuck, had everyone picked up on that? Damn, if everyone could see it so clearly, did that mean Tobias saw it too?

"Ash knows how I feel about Tobias, and he knows how I feel about him."

Logan frowned. "And he's fine with that?"

It was my turn to run a hand over my face, because this was a waste of time and totally irrelevant to the mission. "My love life is none of your business. Getting me to the cure is. Keep your nose and your opinions out of my affairs."

His lips curled menacingly. "You hurt Ash and you'll have me to answer to."

Anger was thrumming through my veins, desperate to be unleashed, and for a moment, Logan was wreathed in a red and purple haze, and then he was crowding me again. Forcing me to back up against the wall with his huge body. Testosterone and vanilla and his warm breath—all too much.

"I mean it, Eva," he said. "Ash is one of the good ones."

Regret, jealousy, grief—the emotions dripped from his words and wrapped around me, suffocating me with their genuine passion. What was this? Were these his emotions?

"I wanted you gone, you know that?" His tone was soft-edged with lethal intent. "As soon as Ash brought you back to the bunker I told Noah you were trouble, but we needed your blood and then you flipped Noah and unleashed his beast. You almost got Ash and me killed over one pathetic human. I was ready to drag you from the bunker kicking and screaming, fuck the blood. But then you had the key and the cure." His lips tightened as if holding back barbed words. "Once we have the cure, once you've served your purpose, we're done with you. I want you out of our lives, do you hear me?"

Ice trickled up my spine at the threat in his voice and the pure menace radiating off him. A day or so ago, I'd have told him to shove it, I'd have told him I didn't intend to stick around anyway, but things were different now. Now there was Ash. Now there was hope and a light feeling in my chest that spoke of new beginnings. Unfortunately, Ash seemed to come as a package deal.

I pressed a hand to Logan's chest hard enough to stem the tremor, hard enough to feel his heart jump beneath my fingers. "Trust me, you're not my favorite person either." My voice came out strong and sure despite the fear blooming in my chest, because we were alone. I was alone with the Fang who'd almost drained me. "But I care about Ash, and I intend on sticking around."

He closed his eyes and grit his teeth and then his hand was wrapped around my throat, tight enough to pin me but not enough to hurt ... not yet. "We don't need you. He doesn't need you."

"Let go of me, Logan." My hand slipped into my

pocket to curl around the penknife I'd found in the kitchen. "Now."

Logan's gaze dropped from my eyes to my mouth and then dragged back up again. "You need to—"

The storage room door slammed open, and Ash stood on the threshold. His gaze went from me to Logan and then settled on Logan's hand around my throat. His mouth turned down, and then Logan was ripped away from me and yanked out of the room.

"Fucking hell, Ash." Logan shoved Ash, but my ogre Fang barely shifted under the assault. "She's not worth it."

Logan wasn't even on my radar when it came to giving a shit, but damn, that stung.

Ash's fist connected with Logan's jaw so fast it made my head hurt. Logan staggered back but didn't go down. Ash's hands spoke terse and stiffly as if he was holding back on violent action.

Logan massaged his jaw. "You know she's in love with someone else, right?"

Ash replied by reaching for my hand and pulling me against him.

"You're a fool, Ash. A fucking fool." Logan backed up, turned, and stormed off.

My pulse was hammering in my throat, hands

shaking from the encounter, and then Ash pulled me into his arms and the tension drained away.

"What is his issue?" My words were muffled against his shirt.

"Not you," Jace said from behind me.

Ash's hold loosened enough to allow me to turn in his arms.

"This isn't about you. Not really," Jace said. He looked to Ash, his gaze speculative. "At least I don't think it is."

"Yeah? Well then you need to tell your brother to sort his shit out, because next time he corners and threatens me I won't be so accommodating." I stepped away from Ash. "We should get going. I'll grab some supplies from the kitchen."

IT WAS ONLY when I was outside the kitchen that I realized I'd forgotten to grab my backpack from my cabin. It contained basic supplies from the main bunker—cereal bars, water, and some protein bars.

Sage was already in the kitchen with two backpacks filled with tins.

I crossed my arms. "You do realize we have to carry those packs for two hundred miles."

"And you do realize that I'm a djinn and could

carry these packs and you for the next five hundred miles. Besides, I need more food than you do."

He hoisted the packs up onto his shoulders. "So, you and Ash?" He wriggled his brows. "Glad to see you took my advice." He made to brush past me but paused to lean in and whisper in my ear, "My offer is still on the table, by the way."

And then he was gone, leaving me slightly aroused and more than a little confused.

Chapter Eight

Three hours on the road and the sun was inching to the apex position in the sky, but we'd agreed to keep pushing on and only stop for a break once we'd navigated the edge of the Wilds.

Jace led the way, map in hand, Ash strode beside me, and Logan and Sage made up the rear. We trekked in silence through a deserted village. The buildings stood silent and abandoned either side of us, forlorn and creepy. A ghost village with not a soul in sight, but that didn't mean there weren't Feral slumbering in the depths of the buildings, hiding from the sunlight.

"We should be coming out of the village and hitting the Wilds soon." Jace glanced over his shoulder but didn't meet my gaze. The awkwardness between us was beginning to grate. It was time to smooth things over.

I lightly touched Ash's arm. "I'll be back in a bit."

Ash nodded.

Picking up my pace, I joined Jace in the lead. We walked in silence side by side for a minute.

Time to start breaking the ice. "How many miles till we hit the Wilds?"

"Another half a mile and we'll be hitting rough terrain. The towns up north are overgrown and wild more so than anywhere else."

"An imbalance in nature?"

"Yes."

"Like the constant full moon."

Jace nodded. "Noah believes that the virus tipped the scales somehow, that the existence of supernaturals on this plane was essential to the balance of our world, and when they turned Feral, that power, that—for want of a better word—magic, leaked into the air, untamed and unfettered. It affected the very fabric of our world."

"Do you think the cure will fix it?"

"I hope so."

It was the longest conversation we'd had since Logan had almost drained me.

Jace folded up the map and shoved it in his back pocket. "I'm sorry, Eva."

"I know. Let's start over."

He glanced across at me, his piercing blue eyes boring into me searchingly. "I'd like that."

A smile curved my lips and the tension in my chest abated. "Can I ask a question?"

"Sure."

"What did you absorb when you fed off me last night?"

He blinked in confusion. "Blood, like the others."

"How is that possible? You just placed your fingers against my skin."

He held up his hands as if trying to figure out how he could have done what he claimed. "I used to wonder the same thing, but when we found the bunker and the lab, Noah did some tests. It turns out that I have microscopic filaments that extend from my fingertips when I'm ready to feed. They pierce the donor's skin and extend into the arteries to draw the blood into me."

"So ... your fingers have thousands of fangs."

He snorted. "I guess they do."

"But you can control it?"

"Pretty much. I mean, if I was starving, dying, then it would be different. But so far, I've been able to control the filaments."

He could feed with a touch, a touch that would incapacitate his prey with euphoria and desire. He could kill someone, and they'd die smiling. Same went for Ash and Logan, but Noah ... with Noah there had been only pain.

"How is it that Noah doesn't have the ability to ... subdue his donor?"

"The endorphins?"

"Yeah."

"Noah's theory was that in the time of the Vladul, there was no need to subdue the donor, because donors were victims. Vladul lived in the shadows, not interested in joining human society and blending in. They were predators who didn't care for their prey's comfort because they had no desire to fit in to society. It was this disregard to fit in that led to their eventual discovery. It was why Noah believes they retreated beneath the earth and fell into slumber; those that remained topside were forced to change and evolve into the Fangs you know today."

"Fangs that lived side by side with humans and who fed but didn't kill."

"Exactly."

And Noah had the Vladul genes. He'd been fighting that nature all his life, trying to be the better man when every instinct in him screamed to just take what he needed. Talk about drawing the short straw.

The landscape shifted from urban jungle to just

... jungle. An explosion of flora greeted us, and the cement and tarmac that had once been the road ahead was completely obscured.

Logan cursed softly under his breath.

"Yeah," Sage said. "The Wilds are something else and they're growing."

"What do you mean?" Logan asked.

"Exactly what I said," the djinn replied. "The square footage that the Wilds cover is increasing. We've been keeping tabs on it over the past decade, and if it continues to expand at the same rate, then fifty years from now there will be nothing but wildland."

I'd heard of the wildlands from Dad—how technology didn't function there, how the laws of physics ceased to matter there. Civilization would be swallowed by nature, and then what?

"Hopefully, the cure will reset the balance," Logan said.

It was our only hope.

The air was thicker here, sweet and almost intoxicating. Blooms, unlike any I'd ever seen, dripped from thick green stems that sprouted up from cracks where the earth had fought back against the man-made constraints of cement and tarmac.

"If this is the edge of the Wilds, I don't even want to see what's in the center."

"No," Sage said solemnly. "You really don't."

The djinn joined us at the head of the group, gently pushing back the flora that blocked our path. The terrain was choked by nature, and any evidence of civilization had been eradicated.

"Are you sure this is the right way?" Logan asked.

Jace studied his compass. "Positive."

"You're lucky we're on the edge of the Wilds," Sage said. "Any farther in and that compass would be useless."

I fell back to walk beside Ash. His arm brushed mine and the contact was reassuring, because all the green and red and orange of nature, all the vibrancy and the aromas that were created to spin my head, were like a noose slowly tightening around my throat.

My hand went up to caress my neck. "Who would have thought nature could be so threatening."

Ash's hand brushed mine and then his huge palm swallowed mine in a gentle grip. My pulse fluttered in my throat. He was holding my hand. We were holding hands. We'd had sex, so this shouldn't be a big deal. Holding hands with a guy wasn't new. I'd held hands with Tobias on several occasions, but we'd usually been running from something, so I guess that didn't count, but this ... this was ... I glanced up at Ash, but his attention was fixed ahead, offering me only his sturdy profile.

And then his brows dropped low in a frown.

"What is it?"

Jace, Logan, and Sage had come to a standstill in front of us.

"What the fuck?" Logan said.

Ash and I drew abreast of the others as my brain pieced together what it was seeing. Twisted metal gates rose up before us, open wide. A hedgerow stood on either side of the gate stretching as far as the eye could see. But it was the thing beyond the gates that had my attention. A huge wheel rose up into the sky, stationary and hung with seats that swayed gently in the breeze. Green and yellow vines hugged the structure and purple blooms lay at its feet. I'd seen this machine in movies on the projector screen at the compound. They'd ridden one in Tobias's favorite film, *The Notebook*.

"Is that a ..." Logan trailed off, canting his head to study the scene.

"Ferris wheel?" Sage said. "Yes, it's a Ferris wheel."

And around it was the rest of the fairground: overgrown booths and attractions and even a dusty, flower-adorned carousel.

"This is weird," Jace said.

No one made a move closer, even though this

was our route. Even though we needed to go forward to get to our destination. If we were going to get to The Shack before the sun went down, we needed to keep moving. This was our shortcut, our way of shaving almost one hundred miles off our journey, but there was something about the scene, a strange element in the atmosphere that brought gooseflesh up on my skin and made my scalp crawl with foreboding. The guys must be picking up on it too. It was danger, it was a warning.

I'd been the one pushing to go through the Wilds, but now ... "Do we have time to skirt the freaky fairground?"

"No," Jace said. "We skirt it and that leaves us in the Wilds after dark."

Ash signed.

"Ash is right," Logan said. "We do not want to be in the Wilds after dark."

Ash's grip on my hand tightened a fraction. This time, when I looked up at him, his gaze was on me, warm and reassuring. We'll be fine, it said. I'll protect you.

My stomach flipped. I protected myself. It was who I was. I'd been trained not to need someone to save me, but damn if it didn't feel good to have the backup. I squeezed his hand in return and together we stepped through the gates into the fairground.

The air rippled over my skin, stinging and soothing at the same time.

"What was that?" Jace sounded shaken.

Sage brushed at his shirt as if dusting it off. "Felt wrong."

Ash stood silent and still, his pale gaze sweeping across the terrain. Yes, there was movement to our right, sending a ripple effect through the viscous atmosphere. Someone or something was beyond the carousel.

"We're not alone here," Sage said.

And then a child's scream tore through the silence.

Chapter Nine

For a second, no one moved, and then we were all running in the direction of the sound. Another scream followed the first but was choked off by a sob. We hurtled around the carousel, past the painted eerie eyes of the horses covered in vines, and skidded to a halt by what looked like a pirate ship suspended in the air.

For a moment, I wasn't sure what I was seeing, and then the woman strapped to the ship by thick green vines came into focus. Her golden hair was awry and her body from the neck down was obscured by creepers. Her arms were pinned to her sides, and dangling from one of them was a child, probably seven or eight years of age. The boy screamed again, kicking his legs as if trying to gain purchase on the air.

"Let go," his mother ordered. "Benji, you have to let go. Drop, roll, and run."

"No. No, Mum. No."

"Benji, this is not a request." It was a tone I'd heard Dad use on more than one occasion. The tone that brooked no argument and one I'd learned to obey without hesitation in the six years we'd been forced to live outside the compound. This boy obviously wasn't familiar with it, because he held firm.

Her eyes grew wide and a low whimper fell from her lips. "Benji, you have to run. Please."

The vines to the left of her rippled and surged and then a face burst forth from them, pale green and shiny with all-too-human eyes. Some of the vines detached themselves from the mass to morph into arms and hands, and then the humanoid thing was crawling toward the woman.

This isn't your problem. Get the hell out of here. Dad's voice was clear as a bell in my head.

You have to help them, Eva. Do something. Tobias? My heart surged. He was with me. Still with me.

I turned to Ash. "Ash, can you get it with your crossbow?"

He was already taking aim.

"Benji. Let go. Let go now!" It was a final command, delivered in an angry bark, and this time the boy acted on instinct.

The fall was at least eight feet, and it was as if

the boy was falling in slow motion, but Logan was a blur, bridging the distance between us and the ship in a blink. The boy landed safely in his arms with a *whoomph* and the woman above us let out a cry of surprise as an arrow *thunked* into the pale green monster. Its scream was a horrific screech. Its body writhed, pinned to the ship, and then the arrow was ejected, leaving the creature unharmed.

"What the hell," Jace said.

The creature was almost on the woman, but I was in motion, running toward the ship, Talwar in hand, no plan, just the need to stop the thing from getting to the woman. The vines … Maybe the vines were somehow connected to the thing. Maybe if I hurt them, I'd hurt it. My sword sliced through the thick green ropes, releasing a pungent stench of rotten things. But the monster didn't even flinch.

"Eva, watch out!" Sage's voice was a boom.

Something whizzed toward me from the left. I ducked on instinct as the creeper rocketed over my head.

"Get back!" Jace called out.

I staggered away from the ship, the little boy's screams ringing in my ears.

"Protect him!" the mother cried. "Please …"

I locked eyes with her, seeing sorrow and acceptance in her red-rimmed gaze, and then the pale green humanoid creature was on her. Its mouth opened to reveal thousands of razor teeth, farther and farther until it was impossibly wide, until it was all mouth and nothing else. Oh, God … Oh, shit. The woman clenched her jaw and closed her eyes. She knew what was coming. I knew what was coming. Look away, fucking hell, Eva, look away. The creature lunged, biting off the woman's head. Her arms jerked as her body convulsed and then she fell limp.

Silence, interrupted only by the rush of blood in my ears and the sickly chomp and slurp of the creature as it ate the woman, surrounded us. Blood dripped and splattered on the ground.

Logan held the boy tight, pressing his head to his huge shoulder to prevent the child from seeing his mother be devoured.

"What the fuck?" Jace's voice shook with emotion.

The vines pulsed around the creature as if benefiting from the feeding. "What is it? What in the world is it?"

"Human," Sage said softly. "Or at least it was once. Now it's just infected." The djinn's tone was laced with sorrow.

"How do you know this?" Logan asked.

"Djinn see things others don't, and at its core,

that thing is human ... was human. Higher brain function has shut down. Now it operates only to feed and survive, and right now, we're prey."

"No, that can't be," Jace said. "Infection kills humans."

"Obviously not in the Wilds," Sage said. "The rules are different here due to the heavy saturation of magic. It seems that infection in the Wilds turns the humans into carnivorous plants."

The plant creature looked up from its meal. Its eyes were clear, lucid, and very human. The mouth had shrunk to a normal size, smeared with crimson and brain matter.

"Fooood," it said.

Low moans drifted up around us, mournful and desperate. Movement to the right caught my eye, and a face burst from the vines wrapped around a huge post with a brass bell on the top. Green eyes gleamed at me, and a scarlet mouth opened wide. The thing on the ship was waking up the others. It was alerting them to our presence, and the last thing we needed was more infected humans.

A sickly shudder ran through me. "Guys, I think we should get out of here. Now."

"Agreed," Jace said. "This way."

He led us away from the ship and back around the carousel at a jog. The little boy's sobs came with us. Logan made soothing sounds, but the child was inconsolable, and his cries were increasing in volume. Nature was everywhere, the infected could be hiding anywhere, and we needed to get the hell out of this fairground before they descended on us.

"Hush," Logan said, struggling to keep hold of the boy.

Dammit. I fell back so I was abreast of Logan and cupped the boy's face firmly in my hands. "Enough. You want to live, then you need to shut up. You cry, they hear you and they will eat you. You got that?"

The boy stared at me in horror.

"That's right. Your mum wanted you to live. So shut up, and you might make it. Cry one more time and we'll leave you behind, you got that?"

It was mean and cruel and harsh, and when his bottom lip trembled I almost lost my stern face. But we had a cure to get, and dying here because we'd tried to save a kid wasn't an option. I'd meant my words. If he compromised the mission, I'd leave him behind.

Eva … no. He's just a kid.

Shut up, Tobias. You idiot. You always do this. You did this with Danny and you did this with Emily. You'd be okay, we'd be together, if you'd just left them behind.

The kid pressed his lips together and nodded.

"Good boy. Your mum would be proud of you."

We were jogging past the Ferris wheel now. Over the soft earth headed north, hopefully out of this hellhole, when the ground around us began to shift and move.

"Shit!" Jace swerved to avoid a whipping vine. It slammed into the earth where he'd been just a moment before, tearing at the soil with the many thorns that decorated it. That could have been Jace, the welt in the earth could have been a welt torn through his flesh.

"Move!" Sage broke into a run.

Ash slowed down as Logan and I came abreast of him, and then he grabbed my hand and we broke into a sprint. The infected rose from the ground, reaching for us with pale green appendages and howling, crimson, razor-lined mouths. They lunged at us from the fairground rides, awakening from a sun-drenched slumber to burst free of the greenery that cocooned them.

The gates out of the fairground were up ahead, too far away, and with the path blocked by infected plant humans, there was no way we'd make it without casualties. A week ago, I'd have accepted this as fact and forged on regardless, caring only for my own survival, but everything was different now. The part of me that I'd subdued for too long, the part that loved and cared and formed bonds, was awake, and she wasn't leaving anyone behind.

The gate was a no-go. "We're not going to make it."

My brain was already working on the problem, scanning our surroundings for a viable alternative to making the gate run, and there it was, sticking out like a sore thumb—a concrete structure marked *mirror maze*. A structure clear of all greenery as if nature itself had shunned it.

I swerved toward it. "This way. Take cover."

The concrete structure loomed closer and then we were bursting through the doors. Ash slammed them closed and bolted them.

"Do a sweep for plant life," Logan said.

"There's none," Sage said. "This place is untouched." He walked past the reception desk and hovered in the doorway to the maze of mirrors. "Empty. Good call, Eva."

The lack of greenery around it had been the tip-off. "But why? Why haven't they grown all over this place?"

"Something in the foundations." Sage ran a large hand over the wall and closed his eyes. "Lead. There are lead rods in the walls, and it's contaminated the soil."

"Lead is toxic to plants," Jace said. He leaned

against a wall and slumped to the ground. "We're safe in here."

My mind was whirring. "The humans are infected, and the infected are usually unable to bear the sun, but maybe because they're plants they need to be alert in the daytime. Maybe come nighttime ..."

"They'll sleep," Jace finished for me, his blue eyes lighting up.

"We wait it out till sunset," Logan said.

It was the last thing we wanted to do, because even though the plant creatures might become inactive, everything else out there that wanted to chow down on us would be awake and very much on the prowl. But what other choice was there?

"Ash?" I looked to the big guy.

He nodded in agreement before heading over to the window that leaked sunlight into the gloom.

Logan carefully set the boy on his feet and walked over to the light switches, flipping them with no result.

The child took a step closer to me. "Mum's dead, isn't she?"

I looked down at him, so tiny and vulnerable, and the urge to shield him was a sharp throb in my temple. But that would be doing him a disservice. If he was going to survive, he needed to toughen up, and the sooner the better.

"Yeah, kid. She's gone. But you're with us now. We're going to take care of you. Okay? But you need to be brave and you need to do as I say."

He nodded, blinking back tears. "Mum was taking me to find others like us."

"Like you? Human?"

He shook his head.

"Claw," Sage said, studying the boy through narrowed glowing eyes. "The boy is Claw, but the gene in him is recessive. It means he can't shift. His mother may have been a full-blooded Claw."

"She would have had to be if her son is a half-blood," Jace said.

We moved away from the boy and dropped our voices.

"I don't understand." I glanced at Jace. "There are no such things as half-blood Claws. Dad would have told me about them."

"Maybe he didn't know about them," Jace said. "It wasn't something that the Claws advertised. Before the infection, Claws were having relation-ships with humans. The government didn't crack down on it because they believed that a human and Claw couldn't produce offspring. They were wrong. Although nothing ever came of a full-blooded male Claw having relations with a human female, if a full-blooded female Claw had relations with a human male, then the resulting offspring was always a half-blood Claw—more human with a recessive Claw gene, unable to shift. Pure Claws could only be created from Claw to Claw procreation."

"What? Were the Claws trying to swell their numbers?"

"No," Jace said. "Claws sometimes fell in love with humans or were attracted to them, that was all."

The boy was standing by the reception desk. I went over and crouched so that we were eye to eye. "Were you headed to Forest Noir?"

He nodded. "Mum thought it would be quicker this way. Dad … Dad was taken by Fangs a few days ago." He glanced warily up at Logan.

"Logan isn't like the Fangs that took your dad."

"He's still a Fang. He needs blood to survive."

"Yeah, but he doesn't want yours."

The boy looked up at Logan for confirmation. The Fang nodded curtly.

Ash was still at the lone window, staring out into the fairground.

"They still there?" Jace asked him.

Ash signed.

Jace puffed out his cheeks. "Okay, we best get comfortable then. We have five hours to kill till sunset."

He laid down his barbed balls and chains. Sage slid his machete from the strap at his waist and placed it on the reception desk. Ash unhooked his crossbow and leaned it against the wall, and Logan unbuckled the sheath holding his spiked bat to his back and dropped it onto the floor before sliding to the ground beside it, back against the wall.

Five hours and then we'd be facing every Claw, Fang, and Feral out there.

Chapter Ten

ELIAS

The tech lab was silent and empty. Almost dawn and many of the Vladul would be retiring for the day. It was an old habit born from our need to hide during the day, not because the sunlight caused us any harm, but because our pale skin and silver hair used to stand out conspicuously, alerting humans to our other-worldness. Hunting at night had simply been easier, but now none of that mattered; it would take time for us to become diurnal.

When we'd first taken over Genesis, Malcolm had ordered the lab to be sealed off, accessible only to essential personnel. It had taken years and the coercion of human scientists to learn what all this meant. But the Vladul were quick studies, and now our own scientists ran the labs. We'd surpassed the humans at their own game but still stumbled against the same blocks they had.

This lab wasn't high security any longer. Most of the discoveries were now old news, and the focus had shifted to bioweaponry, Deanna's expertise, and one which Malcolm had poured all resources into. So, tech sat unused and abandoned, ripe for the picking. Not that anyone would dare. Not until now.

Now where was the thing I needed? Ah, there it was. An inch-by-inch square of black material sat in a glass box with several of its mates—Camoskin, Genesis Foundation's last invention before we'd stepped in and taken over. Humans had been on the verge of creating a new world, one that would have melded supernatural with high-technology. The virus may have decimated the world, but it had created an opportunity for humanity to climb up the ladder and become the apex predator once more. Using the DNA of various animals and supernatural creatures, they'd gone on to create nanotech that could carry runes and enchantments directly into someone's bloodstream in either gaseous or liquid form. They'd created Camoskin, which could mold to any inanimate object and hide it in plain sight, and they'd been on the verge of isolating the element that made creatures like the Claws, Vladul, djinn, and fey so different from humans. An element found only in supernatural beings ... an element called magicka.

They'd been so close to isolating it, and if they had ... It didn't bear thinking about. Vladul scientists had worked around the clock to attempt to complete the work, and thus far, failed.

Thank the ancients.

I plucked a square of Camoskin from the glass box and slipped it into my pocket.

"Elias? What are you doing in this part of the facility?"

I turned to face Gerald with a smile. "Looking for you, actually, and reminiscing."

Gerald was a white coat assigned to this lab with minimal manpower. Malcolm didn't like to be seen as giving up on anything, so a skeleton staff was in operation during the night hours. What they actually did down here was anybody's guess.

Gerald grinned. "Yes. It was fun decoding this work, wasn't it?"

Four months spent assigned to the lab had been far from fun. "Yes. Good times. How is Neela?"

Gerald nodded, enthusiastic now that we were discussing his life-partner. "She's good. And you? Have you met anyone?"

I let out a bark of laughter. "You mean since we crawled out of the earth to take over the human world? No."

He winced. "I suppose it must be hard for you."

He was referring to my royal blood, to the fact that my lineage meant I was predestined for a single soul. He was referring to the fact that Malcolm had killed my bloodline and many of my people, sparing me only to prove that he could be merciful. In doing so, he'd forced the Vladul, who'd once bowed to my family, to follow him. The coup had come a handful of years before we'd been forced underground, and now ... Now he was eager to establish a new rule above ground. My predestined mate was probably dead.

I shrugged. "I could still fall in love."

His smile was close-lipped, polite, because he knew that it was highly unlikely I'd ever fall in love. Maybe lust, but love ... no.

"Not much happening here now," Gerald said with a frown. "Shame. There's so much potential."

Nice change of subject. "Have you made any progress on the magicka isolation?"

Something passed across his face—wariness or fear, it was hard to decipher. He shook his head. "We've been focusing on the Camoskin, actually, trying to make it compatible with mammals."

"Really? Progress?"

"A little. We're about to move to testing phase next week."

My heart rate picked up. "And how does Malcolm feel about that?"

Gerald's throat bobbed. "Oh. I haven't told him yet. I thought we should have some results first ... you know ..."

He was afraid just like so many others, but he wasn't on the roster. He wasn't one of *us* and there was no time to vet him.

"Yes, best to have results before you go to Malcolm." I patted his shoulder, and he tensed.

"What did you really come here for, Elias? Did he send you to check up on me?"

Fear. He reeked of it. "No. I just wanted to reminisce, that was all. How's Brenton? I haven't seen him around lately."

Gerald blinked at me in surprise. "You don't know?"

"Know?"

"Malcolm had Brenton executed three months ago."

The breath whooshed out of my lungs. "I ... I must have missed the memo."

Gerald's lips tightened. "There was no memo. It was all sudden and hushed. Juniper and Frederick were taken too."

"The crime?"

Gerald picked at his coat. "Suspected sedition."

He cleared his throat. "Malcolm believed they had begun a movement against him."

My pulse sped up, but my tone remained light and unaffected. "Really? That's interesting. I wonder what caused him to think that?"

Gerald kept his head down. "I wouldn't know."

It was obvious he was scared to death of Malcolm. He believed I was Malcolm's man and was terrified of what Malcolm could do to him if he said something he shouldn't. But he'd already said enough. Enough for me to know that Malcolm was on to us. He'd killed the wrong Vladul three months ago. How had I missed that? Did he believe he'd prevented the movement?

The next Rising meeting wasn't for another two weeks, but I'd need to get a message to my second before I left to find the key. Deana was working on something for Malcolm. A weapon. Something big. She'd never been good at hiding her smug pride, and her body language had screamed *jackpot*. I was in a race against time and failure was not an option because too many lives depended on me.

Chapter Eleven

The little boy, Benji, dozed on the floor, head pillowed on Logan's backpack. The Fang had been surprisingly gentle with the boy, coaxing him to lie down and smoothing the hair off his brow until his eyelids had fluttered closed. His harsh features softened every time he looked at the child. This was not the Fang I'd come to know and despise. It was disconcerting.

He looked up and caught me staring. "You were too harsh on the boy, you know that, right?"

His words were bites. "I saved his life. You want to wrap him up in cotton wool then you might as well put a bullet between his eyes. If he wants to survive, he needs to learn how."

"She's right." Sage didn't look up from his card

game with Jace. Their hands were blurs as they laid cards faster than my eyes could track.

"Yeah, you would say that," Logan said in response to Sage, his attention still on me. "You do realize he wants to fuck you, right?"

"Shut up, Logan," Jace said. "Enough."

My neck heated but my face remained impassive. "And I'd love a cup of coffee. What has that got to do with anything?"

Sage snorted. "She knows. I laid those cards right on the table straight off. I'm not the type to wrap my feelings in angst."

What did he mean by that?

Silence descended on the group, and Logan stared daggers at Sage. The Fang's pantherine body was wound tight, ready to lash out at the slightest provocation, but the djinn remained focused on his game, not giving Logan the prod he needed. There was something I was missing here, an undertone that didn't quite make sense.

I looked to Ash, propped against the wall opposite me. His eyes were closed, but there was an awareness about him that told me he was far from asleep. He was listening to it all, and he'd act if need be. The fact that he was still and silent was my cue to chill, that and the fact that Jace hadn't even looked at his brother.

Logan's shoulders relaxed, and he dismissed the djinn in favor of the cracked plaster ceiling.

We were all wound tight, that was all.

The sun was making its way across the sky, eating away the hours, hours we could have been using to get to The Shack. This situation was less than ideal, but a journey without setbacks would have put me on edge and left me waiting for the other shoe to drop. At least this way the shit had hit the fan, and we could hopefully come out the other end unscathed. We'd been prepared for the possibility of a night run. Our packs held flashlights and we had our weapons. Hell, the Fangs *were* weapons, able to shift to Claw if needed. We'd be fine, but sitting here and doing nothing was going to drive me crazy. Best to kill time by scoping out the place. See if there was anything we could use outside of here.

I pulled myself up and headed for the stairs behind the reception desk.

"Where are you going?" Logan asked.

"Scout the place out. See if there's anything useful we can grab."

"Forever the scavenger, eh?"

The words were insulting but his tone wasn't, so I let it slide.

I shrugged. "Missed opportunities aren't something I like to cultivate."

He stood. "I'll come with you."

My gaze went to Ash, but he remained unmoved, eyes still closed. Honestly, being alone with Logan was not on my to-do list, but telling him not to accompany me would be admitting that he fazed me, that there was a part of me that was terrified of the menace that he'd shown toward me. Fuck it, if he got grabby, he'd get a fist to the jaw. I was done with his negativity and judgment. I made to turn away, and the air shifted behind me.

I glanced back to find Jace between Logan and me. It looked like Ash might not have any objections, but Logan's brother did.

"Get out of the way, Jace," Logan said with a roll of his eyes.

"No," Jace said. "You can stay here. I'll go with her."

Logan's smile was part sneer. "What's the matter, brother, don't you trust me? Think I'm going to grab a quick snack?"

"Nail on head," Jace said.

Logan's expression smoothed out to iceberg-cold. "I wasn't myself when I almost drained her, what's your excuse? Liked the show, did you?" He leaned in. "You act all righteous and controlled when in reality you're just as bad as me, except *you* get your kicks out of replaying the shit I do in your fucked-up head."

Jace made a grab for Logan's shirt, hands fisting

in the material threateningly. Logan's laugh was derisive.

Sage was on his feet now, ready to intervene if need be.

But Jace released Logan abruptly and dropped his gaze, shoulders heaving. "You really think that." It wasn't a question; it was a desolate statement. "I'm sorry you feel that way."

The heat seeped out of Logan's eyes. His mouth parted to speak, but Jace continued.

"You're wrong, Logan, I'm not like you, and I don't want to be. I hate this craving. I hate this need." His gaze flicked to me, apologetic. "I don't revel in it like you do, and if I could make it go away then I would."

Something dark passed across Logan's face and then his lip curled slightly. "Stop dreaming for the impossible and accept what you are, brother. We're predators, and when we hunt, there is nothing to forgive."

Sage cleared his throat. "I think Ash would like a word?"

Ash's eyes were open and fixed on Logan. He signed something and Logan's body tensed, but Jace nodded.

He licked his lips, his eyes flicking up to the left as he formulated what to say. "Ash says that if you're okay with Logan accompanying you then it's fine."

I looked to Ash; his gray eyes met mine reassuringly. He was giving me control, telling me he trusted my judgment and giving me the opportunity to face the wolf. The last thing I wanted was to be alone with Logan, especially after our encounter in the storage room at bunker one. But there was a part of me that whispered that there was more to the arrogant Fang than met the eye. More to them all.

I focused my attention on Logan, steely and firm. "We'll be fine. And if Logan tries anything, his pretty face won't be so pretty anymore."

Logan placed a hand to his chest. "Aw, she thinks I'm pretty."

I rolled my eyes and headed up the stairs, leaving him to follow if he wanted. The stairwell was too narrow for us to go up side by side, and having Logan right behind me, my butt at his eye level, was disconcerting.

"What's your plan?" he asked as we reached the first floor.

"Plan?" I glanced over my shoulder at him.

"Once you get your friend back? What are you going to do about Ash?"

This again? I was so done with it. "Fuck off, Logan."

DEBBIE CASSIDY

"Classy. But I need to know, seeing as I'll be picking up the pieces when you hurt him."

"You have issues, you know that?" Issues ... Wait a minute. "Is *that* what happened to you? Did someone hurt you?"

His expression closed off, telling me I'd hit the proverbial nail on the head.

"Fuck off, Eva," he said.

My smile was mirthless. "Classy."

Yes, that was it. He'd been hurt in love, and he was now transferring his issues onto Ash and me. I made to head down the corridor, but Logan grasped my elbow and drew me to a halt. His expression was somber and free from malice; it was the only reason I didn't clock him one for touching me. He looked resigned more than anything else.

"Be sure, Eva," he said. "Be sure he's what you want. You need to know ..." He broke off and glanced down the stairs. When he spoke next his voice was low and conspiratorial. "Ash feels things differently from others. He feels more intensely. He will commit himself to you, and he will be there for you regardless of what you decide, because ogres mate for life, and I think ... I think Ash's ogre genes have him seeing you as a mate." He licked his lips and his voice dropped to a strange reverberating resonance. "I need to know what you're really feel-

120

ing. How do you see him? How do you see this working?"

The world was suddenly soft around the edges. Safe and warm and my mind opened like a flower eager to taste the sun. Ash saw me as a mate? As in his one and only. Warmth bloomed in my chest at the word. Yes. That was it, the thing that I'd been trying to identify, the thing between Ash and me — an inexorable bond that had drawn me to him as if he and I were meant to be.

My mouth was moving, and my thoughts spilled from my lips. "I think I feel it too. I don't think I could leave Ash even if I wanted to. I'm hoping Tobias will understand how I feel. I'm hoping that by the time we get him back, I'll have become comfortable with being able to love them both. I've never allowed myself to feel these things and it's new and scary, but I want it. I want Ash and I want Tobias and I think ... I think I may want Sage too."

He blinked sharply, and the spell was broken. The haze retreated, and reality smacked me in the face. My words hung in the air between us, stark and true, pulled from the deep recesses of my consciousness. Thoughts I hadn't been fully aware of.

He'd used his mojo on me.

Anger reared its head, and my hands shot out to shove him away.

"Stay the fuck out of my head, Logan, or I swear I will find a way to hurt you." My voice shook with rage.

He was staring at me with an unfathomable expression. Rage was still thrumming in my chest. I just couldn't be around him right now. I strode off down the dusty corridor, which had several doors leading off it.

"Eva, wait."

"Fuck you, Logan. You had no right to do that."

"To help you understand what you're feeling? I'd say I did you a favor."

"And a foot up the arse would do you a favor, but I've refrained so far."

His low chuckle followed me into the first room, empty except for a couple of overturned chairs and a tool box. Bingo. I crouched and began to rifle through the tools.

"Leave them. They'll just add unnecessary weight to the packs," Logan said.

"Just like your existence adds unnecessary weight to the world."

"Wow, you really don't like me, do you."

Was he serious? "Yep, and I'm pretty certain the feeling is mutual."

Silence greeted me, and then I was hauled up onto my feet and pulled up against his vanilla-scented chest. His brown eyes were light honey in the sunlight streaming into the room, captivating me into silence.

"You think I hate you?" His voice was dangerously low.

My throat tightened. "I know you do."

"Why? Because I didn't want you to stay with us? Because I almost drained you, or because I warned you off Ash. Or is it because I refuse to hide what I am, that I remind you that you're in the company of monsters. That I'm not afraid to admit that it's your blood I want, that it's fucking delicious."

My stomach quivered. "All of the above, actually."

His mouth twisted as if he was in pain and then his lips slanted down over mine. The connection short-circuited my brain and the world was suddenly focused on that point of contact. For a second, there was only the sweet taste of him, the delicious rasp of his tongue, and the questing clash of his teeth against mine. For a moment, my body reacted involuntarily to his, pushing into him, giving him what he needed and taking what it wanted in return. It was violent and sudden—hands fisted in his shirt, his thigh pressed between mine—and then sense came back online. I tore my mouth from his and stumbled away. Distance. I needed distance, because fuck, if I didn't make a rift I'd lose myself in a contradiction of emotion. This was chaos and confusion and no, just no.

"Why did you do that?" My voice was a breathless whisper that grated on my nerves. "Why?" Better. Stronger.

His hand went to his mouth, warm brown eyes slightly unfocused, and then he smiled. "Just as I thought. Definitely not to my taste."

His words were a slap, the cold jet of water I needed to clear away the cobwebs, but I'd be damned if I'd flinch.

I lifted my chin and clenched my fists to hide the tremor in my hands. "The feeling is entirely mutual."

He studied me for a long beat, his gaze speculative, and then he strode from the room. I sagged and pressed my shaking hand to my sensitized lips.

That kiss.

That fucking kiss.

THERE WAS nothing of note in the other rooms, just dust bunnies and shadows, but I lingered longer than necessary, needing to replace Logan's scent with the musty aroma of abandoned rooms, and his touch with the scrape of unsanded wood. It looked like this floor had been a redundant part of the hall of mirrors. There was no point heading into the maze. It would be a waste of time.

If Tobias were here, he'd have coerced me into the maze regardless. He'd have pointed out that we had time to kill so why not have fun doing it. My chest ached with the loss of him. The sooner I got him back, the better. The world and my emotions were a rollercoaster without him to ground me. A change was taking place inside me, one that I didn't fully understand. What if, when we were finally reunited, I wasn't the same Eva as when we'd parted? What if he wasn't the same Tobias? The thought was a vise around my heart.

By the time I headed back down, my pulse and heart rate were steady and unaffected, and the foyer was bathed in hues of red and orange.

Almost sunset.

Ash greeted me with a smile when I returned to the ground floor. He was still seated against the wall, and he arched a questioning brow in my direction.

"Nothing of use up there." My tone was dry.

Logan didn't even look up to greet me. He was sitting beside a wide-awake Benji, his attention fixed on the ceiling once more. Why did that grate?

Jace was by the window staring at the rapidly dimming world outside.

I took a step toward him. "What's it looking like out there?"

"Quiet," Jace said. "No movement."

"That's good."

Benji lifted something off the floor and held it on his lap. A teddy bear? Something wasn't right with this picture.

"Benji ... where did you get that bear?"

Benji glanced down at the soft toy. "This is Pookie. Dad bought it for me."

Ice trickled down my spine. "You didn't have it before ..."

Logan tensed and looked down at the bear. "Did you find it in the toilets?"

Benji nodded. "I forgot it here when we left."

Oh, fuck. "Did you and your mum hide here?"

He nodded. "Mum said it would be safe at night. The plant monsters wouldn't get us in here."

"Shit," Logan cursed. "The fuckers are active at night too."

"Not the same ones." Sage pulled himself off the ground, towering over me. "Moon flowers, no doubt." His jaw was tight. "Should have contemplated that possibility."

I ran a hand over my face as the sequence of events clicked into place. The Claw and her son must have come through the Wilds at night and been chased by nighttime plants. They'd hidden here, thinking that daytime would be safe, like it was from most Feral, but then they'd been attacked by daytime plant people. We'd wasted a whole day only to put ourselves in even more danger.

"We have to go. Now." Logan pulled Benji to his feet.

Benji looked from me to Logan. "Did I do something wrong?"

"No, kid, you did fine," Logan said.

"Everything is going to be okay," Jace said, his voice calm and reassuring.

The kid relaxed, obviously believing the lie. Heck, I almost believed it. But fact was, we were in the shit, like wade-knee-deep in the shit, because now we had fucked-up Feral-human-plant things and the regular Feral monsters to worry about. If we went out there, the odds of us all making it were slim. I'd have to hustle. I'd have to leave them behind.

Yes, Eva, survive. The key is all that matters.

The room was suddenly plunged into darkness, just as a lightbulb went off in my mind.

"We have to fight our way through," Jace said.

He was wrong. "No. We don't. I have a better idea."

Chapter Twelve

TOBIAS

*E*va's face as she'd watched me drive away. Her wide gray eyes filled with devastation. Eva's touch. Her fingers laced through mine at dawn as we fell asleep. Her scent, slightly musky with perspiration but with the undertone of a wild rose.

My heart squeezed painfully.

Hold on. Just hold on.

Her laughter rising like a gentle breeze as we played tag in the halls of the compound. The serious frown on her forehead as she patched up my knee after I scraped it in the compound gardens.

Darkness hovered on the edges of my memory.

No. No. Hold on. Hold on.

"Good, you're doing good." Deana's voice filled my head, bringing me back to reality and flooding my vision with light.

Her face stared at me through the glass between us. "Erasure is progressing smoothly. Could have you wiped in a few hours, but I think I can stretch it to another five sessions before we will have complete memory wipe." She winced. "Sorry about that. It would be easier on you if we just got on with it, but I promised Elias."

Memory wipe? What? What had they taken? God, my head ached. Gray eyes ... gray eyes ...

A door opened behind my tormentor and a man strolled in. Tall and wide-shouldered and silver-haired, he surveyed the lab with mild interest.

Deana backed up and tucked her hair behind her ear. "Malcolm, what a surprise."

"Is it? It shouldn't be. Did you not receive my memo?"

"Memo? No, I mean I haven't checked my email this morning."

Malcolm's golden gaze tracked over her shoulder to land on me. "I can see you've been busy. Can it hear me?"

"No. It's in stasis right now."

Wrong. So wrong. Did she know, or was she lying to him?

"Eerie with its eyes open like that."

"You get used to it," Deana said. "Would you like to see the data?"

"No. I was hoping to have results."

"Results?"

His lip curled. "A weapon ready for deployment. What is taking so long?"

"Erasing a lifetime of memories is a delicate process. If we rush it, we could damage the cortex, and then it will be of no use to us."

"And yet you've managed to erase the other two subjects?"

Deana's shoulders heaved as if holding back a tirade. "Did you read the data I sent over?"

"Excuse me?" Malcolm took a menacing step toward her. "I don't like your tone."

She tucked in her chin. "Apologies. What I meant to say was that the other two subjects are tags. They will be linked to and controlled by Alpha X. This subject was chosen because his brain is perfect for the binding. If we fry him then we may not find another brain like it anytime soon."

"You have two days."

"What? Malcolm, that isn't—"

"While you pussyfoot around, the Claws are growing in number, popping out litters and swelling their ranks. Make it happen, or you'll find yourself on the other side of that glass."

He strode from the room.

Deana's shoulders slumped for a second but then she pushed them back and turned to me. "Looks like we're going to have to accelerate things a little. Fuck. Elias will be pissed."

What did that mean? Erase me. Erase who I was. No.

But she was fiddling with her computer and pressing buttons, and pain lanced through my head.

There she is, the girl I'm going to marry. Neat in her compound school uniform, hair in a ponytail, eyes bright and inquisitive.

"Is this seat taken?"

My mouth is too dry. "Nope."

Her smile lights up the room.

Yes. We will be the best of friends. But even the smile can't stave off the hungry dark.

Wait.

What?

Something … something that needed to be done. Somewhere … needed to be somewhere, and someone … there was someone … someone I needed to find.

Bright light, blue light, green light, red light. Flashes and sounds penetrated my mind. Fire ripped through my fingernails and ran up my arms to settle at my shoulders like smoldering coals, but my scream was trapped in my head.

In my head.

In my head.

Alpha X. Alpha X. Alpha X.

Red light, blue light, green light.
There is a message. A meaning.
Instructions.
Code.
There is metamorphosis.

Chapter Thirteen

I hoisted the mirror up, reflective surface facing outward. The others were watching with questions in their eyes.

"We create a barrier with Benji in the center." I demonstrated walking with the mirror. "We stay out of sight and let them see their own reflections. It should confuse them long enough for us to get the heck out of here."

Jace grinned, his stunning blue eyes crinkling at the corners. "They have no higher brain function, which should mean we can pull this off. Good thinking, Eva."

Yeah, getting out of scrapes seemed to be my forte.

Sage grabbed a mirror and hoisted it up, his brow crinkled in a frown. "This is heavy."

"Aw, are all those muscles just for show?" Logan jibed.

Sage ignored him, his gaze fixed on me. "Eva … how are you holding one up?"

It was heavy but not unmanageable. "This one's probably not as heavy as yours."

He set his mirror down and reached for mine. I relinquished it and watched his face as he hoisted it up.

"No. It's the same weight."

Logan picked up a mirror and then glared at me accusingly.

I looked from Sage to Logan. "What?"

"Either you're freakishly strong, or you're not what you say you are," Logan said. He set the mirror down and stalked toward me, but Ash intercepted him with an arm.

Logan's jaw ticked, and he turned his head to look at Ash. "She's hiding something. She has to be."

"Why?" Jace asked. "Why does she have to be hiding anything?" He sounded genuinely perplexed.

Logan inhaled sharply. "Forget it." He backed off.

"No. Answer him." I crossed my arms.

"I don't want to," Logan said.

Jace looked uncomfortable.

Sage's smile was revelatory. "Ah, yes. I remember, it's because you can't lie, can you?"

Logan's expression was murderous. "Fuck you, Sage, and fuck Noah for sharing that with you."

Ash's hands spoke.

"Ash says we need to get moving," Jace said. "He also said some curse words, but I'd rather not repeat them."

Sage broke eye contact with Logan, dismissing the Fang in favor of me. "I'm sorry, I sometimes underestimate human ability. We should get going."

He was attempting to brush this under the carpet, but now that he'd mentioned it, the question was like a barb in my mind. How the heck could I lift as much as them?

DEATH WAITED OUTSIDE THE DOORS. I closed my eyes briefly and took a steadying breath. "Stay together. Benji, stay in the center. You got that?"

"Yes, Eva."

"Good."

I stared at Sage's broad back. He was at the door, ready to fling it open.

Okay, we could do this. "On the count of three. One. Two. Three."

Cool air rushed into the building and then we

were marching out into the bright night. Moonlight reflected off the mirrors that created a barrier around us.

"Stay together," Sage ordered.

I walked sideways, peering through the gaps between my mirror and Sage's. Darkness writhed just out of reach. They were coming. They could sense us. If the mirrors didn't throw them off, we were done for.

"Incoming at six o'clock," Jace said from the rear.

"Three o'clock," Logan said.

Damn, they were zeroing in on us all right. "Faster. We need to move faster. Benji, grab hold of my shirt."

We broke into a jog with Sage as our eyes and the infected plant humans closing in. The air was suddenly thicker and cloying. Benji coughed. They were releasing spores or something into the air. My throat began to close, and the edges of the world darkened.

Benji's grip slipped.

It had to be a toxin to disable us. "How far?"

"A couple of meters."

Benji hit the ground.

Leave him.

No. "Cover me." I dropped my mirror and hauled Benji into my arms. The world was a foggy haze. It wouldn't be long before I hit the dirt. "Run!"

I broke cover, sprinting for the wavering gates. Black vines attacked, hacked off by Sage's machete before they could grab me. Screeches and strange gurgling sounds tore the air, and then I was through the gates and beyond. Knees met earth and my lungs rebelled, leaving me gasping and spluttering.

Benji. Shit. He wasn't breathing. Shit.

"Eva." Sage fell to his knees beside me as I began CPR on the boy.

Leave him, you're wasting time.

Damn you, old man.

"They're coming." Jace skidded to a halt beside us. "They're coming through the gates."

Benji took a gasping breath and opened his eyes.

"Thank God." Sage scooped the boy up in one arm and grasped my elbow with the other. "Can you stand?" He tugged me up.

My knees wobbled.

"Fooood …"

Ash picked me up and threw me over his shoulder, and we were back on the run. The air *whooshed* by and branches snagged in my hair, yanking painfully as if attempting to hold us back. My lungs wheezed as they recovered from the toxin the plants had pumped into the atmosphere.

"They've dropped back," Jace reported.

We reduced our speed down to a jog.

"Keep moving," Sage said. "Jace, are we headed in the right direction?"

"No. We're off track," Jace said. "We'll exit the Wilds in about two miles and then have to skirt the Wilds to get to The Shack."

The very thing we'd hoped to avoid, but I'd take Feral, Fang, and Claw over these toxin-pumping Feral humans any day.

The air was clearing, and the feeling was returning to my legs when the whispers started.

Stay.

Turn around.

Stay.

Close your eyes and rest.

Shit, my eyelids began to droop.

"Don't listen," Sage ordered. "Focus on walking. We're almost there."

Come to me. Touch me.

Desire jumped under my skin and then flooded my body. Ash's arm tightened under my butt, his muscles tensing at every point of contact.

Need me, want me. Touch me. Feel me.

Oh, God, what was that? Heat traveled down my abdomen to the juncture of my thighs.

"Fuck." Logan's voice sounded thick with desire.

Beneath me Ash's chest was heaving in time to my throbbing sex.

"Focus on something else," Sage ordered. "Don't let them in your head."

"What are they?" Jace's tone was breathless.

"Remnants," Sage said.

"Remnants of what?"

"The lonely dead."

"Ghosts?" Logan said, incredulous. "Are you saying the fucking Wilds are haunted?"

"Souls are energy, and those that died in this twisted place are trapped. Over time, they have become hungry for vengeance. They can't hurt us, but they can get in our minds and manipulate our actions."

So, they wanted me to get horny? That made no sense unless we were all hearing something different. "What do you hear?"

Sage was silent, but Ash's grip on me tightened, almost possessively.

It was Logan that answered, his words laced with anger. "It's telling me to fuck you. To rip you from Ash and take you up against that tree up ahead."

Ash's growl was a menacing sound that had the hairs on the back of my neck springing to attention.

"Same," Jace said softly.

"Sage?" My voice trembled.

"It wants us to fight over you, and kill each other

139

to get to you," Sage said. "But that's not going to happen."

The guys picked up the pace as the whispers intensified, as my body ached to be claimed, as I ground myself against Ash's shoulder. They penetrated my mind, claws digging in, tearing moans from behind my clenched teeth.

"Give her to me," Logan said.

Ash stumbled, and I slipped from his grasp. Other hands grabbed at me, pulling me away from Ash. Ash let out a roar that was cut off by the thud of fist meeting flesh.

Hands on my breasts, lips on my neck, hardness between my thighs, the world was topsy-turvy with welcome sensation. Lips on mine. Vanilla, sweet vanilla. Deep cocoa eyes sucking me in, drowning me in sensation that wrapped around my heart and squeezed.

"Mine," Logan said. "Can you feel it?"

How was he speaking to me? His mouth was on mine, tongue sliding against mine.

A flutter in my chest. An awakening. No. What was this?

"It's there. It's really there." The kiss deepened.

"Get a grip, Logan." Sage's voice was deeper than usual, cutting through the haze of euphoria surrounding me.

Logan was torn away from me, and Sage stood

before me. His fiery eyes pinned me to the spot and ignited a fresh wave of desire inside me. The whispers were in my head, urging me on, begging me to take what I needed.

Sage's lips called to me, his powerful body ached to be touched. I reached for him, and he took a step back.

"No, Eva, not like this." He blinked hard and shook his head.

"Please ..." I reached for him again but never made contact.

The world tipped, and I was staring at the ground as it rushed by.

Fuck me. Inside, deep inside me.

And then the voices stopped. Just like that.

Oh, God. What ... I'd almost ... Heat bloomed in my face. Ash carried me, his body tense beneath me, and damn if I didn't still want him. I needed to be on my feet, to not be touching him right now, because even though the voices had stopped, every inch of me was on fire with need.

I tapped his back. "I can walk. I'm good."

Ash stopped and lowered me down the length of his body, tightening his grip when my mouth grew level with his. His silver eyes scanned my face, and then his lips crushed mine in a kiss that channeled all the frustration from the last half hour. My back met the bark of a tree, and I wrapped my arms around his neck, opening for him, deepening the kiss and sucking on his tongue in an imitation of what I'd like to be doing with his manhood. For a moment, it was just him and me. His cinnamon taste filled my mouth, his taut thigh rubbed against my wetness, and his thick fingers bit into my hips.

"So, it's okay to get him off?" Logan strode past. "How about a little consideration for the rest of us with a fucking hard-on."

Ash broke the kiss and bared his teeth at Logan. The Fang backed up, hands in the air, his mouth turned down, but my body was reacting—that flutter in my chest again. It intensified when Logan's warm brown eyes met mine, sucking the breath from my lungs, and then he broke contact and walked away. Breathe, Eva, just breathe it away.

Sage strode past, his profile like stone as he forged ahead, as if he couldn't get away from the last few minutes fast enough. Jace followed, keeping his gaze averted from us. I'd have let them ... if they'd tried to ... shit.

I tucked in my chin, reining in all the feels and the embarrassment, and carefully extricated myself from Ash. I stood on tiptoe and pressed a kiss to his jaw, inhaling his cedar scent to ground me.

His gaze was still scorching, telling me he was far from done. It flipped my stomach and stole my breath. Once this was all over ... once we were all safe ...

He took my hand and we jogged to catch up with the others.

THE WILDS PARTED before us and spat us out into the broken world. The voices were far behind and everyone's libido seemed to have recovered, and yeah, we wouldn't be revisiting that scenario again.

"I never thought I'd be this happy to see tarmac," Jace said.

A brief breather to get our bearings and we were on our way again. Benji rode Sage's back, clinging to the huge djinn like a rhesus monkey, but his eyes were drooping, and it wouldn't be long until he fell asleep.

"Jace, how many miles?"

"Five miles. We should do it in an hour."

Too long. "The kid won't stay awake that long. We need to make a sling for him."

"We can just take turns carrying him to our chests," Logan said.

"And if we get in a fight?"

"She has a point," Jace said.

Our boots crunched over gravel pushed up by

green shoots—innocuous shoots because we were no longer in the Wilds, but still.

Logan swung his backpack around as he walked and began rifling through it. A sheet and a belt and we had a nifty sling to anchor Benji to Sage's back. This was working. We may actually make it to The Shack without any further mishaps. Hope, the enticing whore, dropped me a wink, but fate, the treacherous cow, decided she'd do one better and blow me a kiss, because in the next moment howls rose up to the east.

Distinctive and close.

Feral Fangs.

Chapter Fourteen

ELIAS

My forte was tracking, and even a cold trail could burn hot under my gaze. The starting point had been the office building where I'd first set eyes on her — hair the color of wet sand bathed in a midday sun, and eyes like a sky just before a storm. The defiant set to her jaw and the gleam of determination in her eyes had teased my pulse. She'd moved like silk, like a dancer that heard a beat we couldn't. For a moment, I'd been captivated, and then the reality of the situation had set in and instinct had taken over.

She'd fought well. If she hadn't then she'd be dead. And then there had been the key nestled against her breastbone. Tanned, velvety skin …

I blinked and focused on the road ahead, on the purr of the motor beneath me.

The key. This was about the key, and the trail from the warehouse had led me onto this road. There'd been a stop off on the side of the road where the air reeked of shit and decay. Maybe they'd regrouped there, but then the tire tracks had led north.

Where was she headed? Was she even in the van? It was a gamble, but it was a worthy one.

The van's tracks glowed in the growing gloom just for me. My gift. My ability. If she was in this van, then I'd find her. But then the tracks swerved and ended.

I brought my bike to a halt and stared at the road ahead, studying the burn marks. The van had braked hard. Something had forced them to stop.

My heart beat faster. What if she was hurt?

I blinked hard. Of course, her welfare mattered. She had the key, after all. Leaving my bike propped at the side of the road, I headed toward the scorch marks. Inhale and visualize. Scents, so many scents. Djinn ... There had been djinn here. Had they taken her? I reached up to rub away the sudden ache in my chest. Her scent, I'd taken her scent and it was hidden in my memory, easily summoned when visualizing her heart-shaped face.

Sunshine, she reeked of it, with an undertone of musky heat and wildflowers. Ignoring the tightening in my loins, I set to catching her scent. Here and here. Yes. Time to track.

THE BIKE WAS STILL on the side of the road but invisible to the naked eye under its Camoskin. It would be safe until I returned, but right now my attention was fixed on the camp that glowed eerily in the moonlight. Wards shimmered pale blue in the sky, and an electric tang tainted the air. Feral would steer clear of the anomaly. A clever ploy by the djinn to protect themselves and their human companions. Movement and sound. Was she here? Her aroma had led me here, but there was no going farther, not without being discovered.

Inching closer, but remaining in the shadows, I focused on the sounds coming from beyond the wards.

"Sleep now."

"One bedtime story only."

"Yes, like that, just like that. Oh, Vince. Oh, yes."

"—human girl associating with Fangs takes our leader and you're okay with that?" a male voice queried.

This one. This was the one.

"You don't believe their story?" a female replied.

"I don't know what to believe," the gruff voice said. "All I know is that we're ready to act now, but it will take at least five days for them to reach the mountains. They'll have to skirt the Wilds to get to the road leading to the Lake District, and you know what kind of shit populates the north. I think we should—"

"Wait," the female said.

"What?"

"There's something out there. I can feel it."

Shit. Time to back up. But I had what I needed. I had a direction. I'd catch her scent, and I'd find her.

Chapter Fifteen

Another howl drifted toward us, closer this time.

Logan and Ash exchanged glances, and then Ash signed at Logan.

Logan nodded. "We're going to do this in Claw form," he said. "You and Sage keep moving. Look for the sign for the service station, and then take the dirt track. The Shack is on the basement level. There's an entrance at the back of the building that should be safe. We'll meet you there."

"Your weapons?" Sage asked.

Logan smiled. "They'll stay with us."

They'd done this before—appeared clothed and carrying their weapons after a change. I'd have to get details on how that worked once we were safe.

Right now, we needed to run because the howls were getting louder.

"Get going," Jace said. "We'll cut them down. And Eva, you need to keep them off Sage."

Benji was fast asleep against Sage's back, unaware of the threat. Let's hope he stayed that way. The Shack was still an hour away.

"Can you sprint with Benji on your back?"

Sage's smile was a slow-burn *fuck yeah*.

We broke into a run, and I pulled ahead, having to slow down for him to catch up.

"You move fast for a human," Sage said.

Did I? I'd never noticed before. The revelation niggled at the back of my mind, brushed aside by the howls now right on top of us.

Snarls and growls joined the Feral Fang screams. The guys had made contact. No time to stop and look. No time to turn around. We needed to get Benji to The Shack. Logan had said they'd be right behind us, and I needed to make sure the Feral stayed off Sage's back.

"You want to go back and fight, don't you?" Sage said.

"What gave it away?"

"You're wreathed in red."

"I hate that you can see right through me."

"No, you don't." His voice was warm honey.

He was right. I didn't. Another weird thing to

ponder. The world rushed by as we sprinted without breaking a sweat, without a gasp or a burn in the lungs. What was this? What was happening to me?

"Eva, two o'clock."

The Feral Fangs loped low to the ground, their leathery skin painted gray by the moonlight, bald heads gleaming. There was no way we'd outrun them, there were too many of them. They'd flank us, cut us off, and then we'd be done for.

I skidded to a halt. A quick glance behind me showed a bare stretch of road. The guys were out of sight, probably still fighting the first Feral batch. Dammit, the Wilds was looking rosy about now.

"Take the boy," Sage ordered. "I can handle this, but you need to take him."

"What are you going to do?"

He turned his head slightly, one eye fixed on me, and then the corner of his mouth quirked up. "I'm going to show them how hot I am."

Fire ... Of course, he had fire literally at his fingertips. "Why didn't you use it in the Wilds?"

"Just take Benji." He turned away, offering me the child.

The boy moaned softly in his sleep as I used my newly acquired penknife to cut the bindings holding him to Sage. He tumbled into my arms, still asleep. Damn, he must be exhausted.

"Go," Sage said. "I'll be right behind you."

The Feral were almost on us, and even though every inch of my body screamed at me to stay and fight, the tiny bundle of vulnerability in my arms forced me to turn and run. Heat blasted my back and hot air pushed me forward. The Feral howls were cut off and the smell of burnt flesh filled the air. *Crackle, pop, fizz.*

The stench hit the back of my throat, and I came to a stop, gagging and choking. Benji stirred but didn't wake up. Fuck, it reeked. I looked back to see Sage's silhouette against a wall of fire. Figures danced in the flames, twisting and pirouetting to the tune of death. He'd done it. He'd annihilated them.

And then the huge djinn dropped to his knees.

Shit.

Benji moaned. "Mum?"

"No, kiddo, it's Eva." A quick glance back at Sage. He was slowly toppling to the side. "You need to wake up, Benji. That's right. Up."

I glanced around desperately, trying to find somewhere safe to stash him for a minute. The tree line loomed to the left. Yes, a tree.

"Eva, what's happening?" Benji rubbed his eyes with his fists.

I strode over to the nearest tree. "You ever climb a tree, kid?"

He nodded.

"Good." I helped him into the branches, and he

began to scramble up. "You stay there, you stay hidden. I'll be back for you."

"Promise." His voice trembled.

I locked gazes with him. "I promise."

Tearing away from his frightened face, I ran back toward Sage. He was on the ground now, lying still. The wall of flame had eaten away at the Feral wave, but it was dying rapidly. Enchanted flame shelf life probably wasn't too long. It was probably meant to hit its target, turn it to cinder, and be done.

"Sage." I shook the big guy's shoulder. "Sage, can you hear me?"

Nothing.

He was out cold. Had using his power knocked him out? It would explain why he hadn't used fire in the Wilds. Several more Feral howls lit up the air beyond the flames. He'd got a bunch of them, but it looked like there were more headed our way. More waiting for the flames to die down. Damn, he was heavy, but I managed to hoist him into a sitting position. Come on. I'd lifted a huge mirror for God's sake, I could carry a djinn. Muscles straining, I almost had him in a fireman's lift when the fire went out.

The Feral hovered beyond the line of scorched earth for a moment, as if stunned by the turn of events. Slowly, carefully, I lowered Sage back to the ground and then fluidly pulled my Talwar from its sheath.

Thanks for waiting, guys.

The Feral attacked, and I met them head-on, dancing around Sage to cover the djinn with my blade. No time for music in my head. Didn't matter. There weren't that many Feral—five, no, six ... Wait, seven. Done. We were done. But the howls in the distance told me more had been attracted by the blood and carnage. Parasites, bloodsucking fucking parasites.

I dropped onto Sage, straddling his hips, and shook him with everything I had. "Sage." I slapped him hard.

There was no way I could carry him fast enough. There was no knowing how many were headed this way. I was good, but not invincible, and there was Benji to consider. Could Feral climb trees?

Sage's face was calm and serene in repose, my handprint fading into his tanned skin. His lashes were inky fans against his cheeks and that mouth that liked to laugh and tease was slightly parted. I ran my fingers across his lips.

"Damn you, Sage. Damn you." My voice was grit and indecision.

The Feral's bloodcurdling screeches were closer now. Minutes away. I'd have to leave. I'd have to leave him here to die.

I pressed my hands to his chest, anger a mini tsunami in my chest. "Damn you!"

The rage, hot and potent, rushed down my arms and slammed into him. His body lit up amber beneath his clothes for a second, and then his eyes popped open and his gasp tore the air.

"Sage?"

He stared at me, at my hands on his chest, and then his fingers curled around my wrists. "What did you do?" His gravelly voice was tinged with awe.

"I … I don't know. I …"

He sat up quickly, so we were chest to chest. "Feral are coming." His breath caressed my lips, leaving them aching for the pressure of his mouth, but some other awareness pricked at my skin.

"They've shifted direction." I scrambled off him. "Get Benji. He's in the tree up ahead. Get him and get to The Shack. I need to go back. I need to warn the others they have incoming. The Feral are upwind; the guys won't smell them coming."

Sage pulled himself to his feet, looking torn.

I held up my sword. "I got this."

He inhaled through his nostrils, nodded, and backed up, his gaze on my face. "We talk. Later …"

"Later."

We turned away from each other and ran in opposite directions. My boots left soft thuds in my wake, and the sounds of ripping and tearing grew nearer and then the guys came into view, highlighted by a proud moon—three massive figures tearing up the night. The final Feral dropped, and they turned to face me with snarls.

Terror flashed through me at the sight of their monstrous forms, but then their lips dropped over their snarls, and they lowered their heads. My heartbeat slowed. Ash, Jace, and Logan. These were the guys. Golden and silver and obsidian wolves. Fangs.

I walked up to them. "More are on their way, upwind. We need to go. Now."

Ash raised his golden head, silver eyes glinting where the moonlight caught them. He sniffed the air, and then growled low in his throat. Jace looked to the tree line, and padded a few steps toward it, his sleek silver body dappled with Feral blood stark against the night.

I followed behind him. "A shortcut?"

He nodded his huge head.

"We can lose them. Is there water?"

His head bobbed side to side, unsure.

"Let's go."

Jace led the way off the road and into the murky woodland. Slender, wicked branches stabbed at my skin and snagged my clothes. The wolves ran at my side, flattening the ground with their paws with each bound. The wind whipped through my hair, raking at my scalp, and for a moment there was nothing but Jace's silver form ahead like a beacon, Ash's golden bulk to my left, Logan's sleek black form to my right, and the melody of freedom in my blood. Ash turned his head my way, and I swear, he looked like he was grinning at me, tongue lolling slightly.

Eyes on the path, Eva.

Jace leapt into the air, and I followed instinctively, scaling a fallen tree trunk with ease and landing lightly on my feet. The air was moist here with a significant tang that signaled water. Sure enough, the rushing sound of a river hit my ears a minute later.

Track through water, and wash off the blood, wash off the scent.

Jace hit the water first, his silver body diving down and coming up clean of the crimson splashes of Feral blood. Logan and Ash met the water at the same time as me, swimming either side of me like lupine bodyguards.

The earth was moist beneath my boots as I scrambled out. The chilly air slapped my soaked skin, and my teeth were instantly chattering. No sign of the Feral behind us. Thank goodness, we may have lost them.

Up ahead, Jace was shaking himself dry. Oh, shit.

"Wait!" I held up my hands, too late, as Ash and Logan chose that moment to shake off the water clinging to their fur.

Double soaking. Shit, my lungs ached.

Ash nudged me with his nose and then jerked his head, indicating his back.

"You want me to ride you?"

Logan made a strange choked sound. Dirty bastard. I climbed up onto Ash's back, clamped my thighs into his side, and slid my fingers deep into his fur before clenching my fists. Thick, golden silk. Is this what his hair would feel like if it was longer in Fang form?

He chuffed in question.

"I'm good."

And then the ground was flying beneath us and the woodland was thinning out. A shadow loomed up from beyond the trees. A three-story building. The service station, a place where travelers would have stopped to refuel, shop, or sometimes stay the night. This was our haven for the rest of the night.

We'd made it.

Chapter Sixteen

The Shack was a sporting goods store at the basement level of the service station. We entered via the hidden exit Jace had told us about and onto a fire exit. A flight of metal stairs brought us onto the basement floor, dark and abandoned, and using flashlights we found our way to The Shack.

Sage was already there. He'd made a nest for Benji using sleeping bags, and the kid was already asleep again. The djinn stood up hastily at our arrival, eyes aglow.

I waved him back down. "Relax. We're all accounted for."

"And the first thing we need to do is get Eva's clothes off," Logan said.

Ash shoved Logan hard. The dark-haired Fang staggered back, hands up, grin on his face.

I grabbed Ash's shoulder. "He's right, Ash. I need to get out of these clothes, or I'll catch a chill."

Ash's shoulders tensed. He signed rapidly and then stalked off.

"He said there are changing rooms at the back of the store and to meet him there," Jace said.

But my attention was on Logan. "That wasn't funny." I headed toward the back of the store.

"It so was." Logan trailed after me. "You should have seen his face. I thought he was going to hit me. He's going to love sharing you with Tobias."

My cheeks flushed. "I don't want to talk about it." Thank God, there was the changing room with the half door and hopefully a fucking lock.

"That's right, just bury your head in the sand," Logan drawled. "You know the more time you spend together, the stronger his feelings are going to get, right?"

I stepped into the cubicle, and he slammed the palm of his hand on the door to stop me shutting it in his face.

He canted his head. "It's happening to you too, isn't it? Not just with Ash, though ..." He stepped into the cubicle, forcing me back against the wall and trapping me in the cage of his arms. "You felt something back there in the Wilds when I kissed you."

"Yeah, I was horny, we all were. It didn't mean anything."

"And what about in the hall of mirrors? Were you under a horny spell there too?" His tone was far from teasing now. It was probing and invasive.

Why did he give a shit? "You caught me off guard."

"So off guard that you kissed me back for a full thirty seconds?"

"Wow, you were keeping count. Sexy."

The corner of his mouth quirked. "I am, aren't I?"

I breathed a sigh of relief; this cocky Logan I could handle. "And arrogant and full of himself."

His brown eyes darkened so they were almost black, and dark veins radiated out from them. Hunger. This was hunger.

"What is happening to you, Eva?" His voice was thick with need. "What's happening to us?"

The question knocked my bravado on its ass, because yes, there was something different about me and it had begun as soon as I'd been picked up by Ash, as if a door inside me was slowly being dragged open. But I wasn't ready to examine what lay beyond it.

I shoved at his chest, but he was unmovable

muscle. "It's not feeding time yet, and the only thing happening to me is that I'm freezing my arse off."

Ash's scent drifted over Logan's shoulder. Thank God he was back. Logan didn't move for a long beat, keeping me trapped in the cage of his arms, and then he smiled thinly and stepped out of the cubicle to be replaced by Ash.

The silver-eyed Fang looked at me questioningly, like, *do I need to kick his arse?*

I shook my head. "I'm fine. Just cold."

He handed me a bundle of clothes and then stepped out of the changing room. Logan was still standing outside, arms crossed.

"Thank you, Ash." I shut the door firmly.

"Spoilsport," Logan said.

I quickly stripped out of the wet clothes and pulled on the dry, slightly too large ones. Gray joggers and a long-sleeved polo top. Going commando felt weird but there was no way I was keeping the sopping wet knickers on. The men's clothes hung off me, but damn it felt good to be dry. Ash was standing outside the room when I opened the door. He scooped up my wet things and wrung them out so they were almost dry. He held up my panties. And arched a brow.

I smacked his shoulder, unable to keep the smile off my face, and then he was stepping into my space, crowding me with his body until we were against the wall. He hoisted me up, and I wrapped my legs around his waist. We remained like this, eye to eye, for a long beat, and then he rubbed the tip of his nose against mine and brushed his lips across my mouth. He pulled back, his pale eyes all pupil. My heart felt too full, and three words sprang to my lips. I bit down on my bottom lip to stop myself from saying them, because despite this strong connection, despite this need to be in each other's gravitational fields, it was too soon. We barely knew each other, and once those words were out, there was no taking them back. I wanted to, *needed* to be sure.

His eyes crinkled, and his mouth moved—three little words that crushed the air from my lungs and brought tears to my eyes.

I exhaled sharply. "Damn you, Ash. Damn you for saying it."

He gently lowered me to the ground and walked away.

Ash had pulled out more sleeping bags and a battery-operated lamp. We'd made camp at the back of the store, placing the lamp in the center like a campfire and positioning our bags around it. Energy bars and water had been consumed and now Ash was asleep to my right and Sage lay dozing to my left. Logan was snoring softly opposite, but Jace was wide awake staring at the lamp as if it were an actual campfire.

I climbed over Ash to sit by him. "Penny for your thoughts?"

He smiled. "Just wondering what a 'normal' world will be like."

"Well, right now, *this* is normal."

He chuffed. "Yeah, I guess it is. I just ... I'm wondering where we'll fit in once the virus has gone."

"You mean supernaturals?"

"No. I mean me and the guys. The experiments that shouldn't exist. Once the dust settles, and the humans and natural supernaturals find their niches again, where will that leave us?"

"Your existence may have been manipulated, but you're not a threat. You're a new breed, and that's kind of exciting."

"It doesn't work that way, or at least it didn't. I've done my research into the past, into what the world was like. Supernaturals stick to their own. They thrive on factions. The vamps stick with the vamps, the Claws with the Claws, the fey to the fey, and so on and so forth. Where does that leave us?"

He had a point. "Dwelling on it now is a waste of mental energy. When the time comes, we'll deal with it." I grinned. "And having a hand in saving the world should give you major brownie points."

He ducked his head to hide a smile. "Always the practical one, aren't you?"

I shrugged. "It's a darned curse."

He gnawed on his bottom lip. "Look, I'm sorry about the way Logan's been acting."

"You mean his hot and cold attitude toward me?"

He nodded. "I wasn't going to say anything, we agreed not to, but maybe if you know the truth you can stop yourself from despising him so much."

My curiosity sat up, ears perked. "Go on."

"A few years back there was a girl ..."

"Aha, I knew it. Logan was hurt by her, right?"

He blinked across at me. "God, no. If only that was it." He licked his lips. "Julia was ... She was beautiful, inside and out. We saved her from a Feral Claw attack, and she ended up staying with us at the bunker. She offered to feed us and she ... She became more than a donor to us all."

My pulse skipped. "You were sleeping with her? All of you?"

Jace squeezed his eyes shut. "When you put it that way it sounds sordid, but it wasn't like that. We loved her, and she loved us. We were happy." His tone was choked.

My scalp prickled because obviously something

had gone wrong, something had happened to her, because she wasn't with them any longer. "What happened, Jace?"

He met my gaze with dull blue eyes. "Noah killed her."

Chapter Seventeen

Noah killed her ...

His words took a second to process. "What? Why? How?" Even as the words fell from my lips, my mind solved each question. "He lost control, didn't he?"

Jace ducked his head. "It was awful. When we found her ... When we found them, she didn't even look like herself anymore. She was a husk. He drained her dry, Eva. Every last drop. And the fucked-up thing is, when we found her, she had her arms around his neck, as if in her final moments, she'd simply submitted to her fate." He shook his head. "I don't even think she fought him."

The fool had thought he would stop, that he would come to his senses. She'd believed that love was enough.

"Shit, Jace. I'm so sorry."

It explained a lot. It explained the animosity between Logan and Noah. It explained the little digs, and why Logan kept warning me off Ash. An ugly, twisted emotion filled me.

"Did Ash love her too?"

Jace smiled softly. "Ash loved her, Eva. He was kind to her, but it was nothing like the way he is with you. He was never instinctively territorial with Julia. Julia grew on him over time, but it seems with you, the attraction, the emotions have grown exponentially. You seem to have activated his ogre genes. "

The pinch in my throat eased. So what if Ash had been with someone else. They all had, but that was before my time.

"Logan loved Julia from the start," Jace said. "He was a different Fang around her, and Julia loved him back. She said she loved us all the same, but it was obvious that she loved Noah the most."

"And you? How did you feel about her?"

His smile was lopsided. "I was head over heels for her. For that year and a half she was with us, she became my world. It almost destroyed us when she died. Logan blamed Noah for a long time, but eventually they began speaking again, and we agreed that we would never form that close a bond with another female again. Her death almost killed

Noah and Logan's relationship. Gina was the perfect pick. From the start, we all knew there would never be more to our relationship with her than feeding. But with you ..." His gaze traversed my face. "When Ash brought you back, we knew you were dangerous. If we weren't starving for blood, we'd have let you go immediately. When you set the temporary terms to our agreement, it was a relief. But now ..."

"Now Logan is concerned that I'll hurt Ash. That if something happens to me, then Ash will be broken."

Jace frowned. "Well, that's a part of it, but surely you realize that the main reason is—"

The backpack beside Jace crackled with static. Jace scrambled to get it open just as Noah's voice, clear and comforting, poured out of it.

"Jace, Logan, come in. Over."

Jace grabbed the radio and depressed the talk button. "Hey, Noah. I'm here. Over."

"How are things going? You should be at The Shack by now. Did you make it okay? Over."

How to answer that? Luckily for me Jace had the radio. "We made it fine, Noah. A couple of hiccups on the way, but we're all accounted for. Over."

A beat of silence. "Why do I get the impression a couple of hiccups amounts to fighting for your lives.

I'm glad you're all right. I wish I could be with you. Over."

"We miss you too," Jace said. "Just a few more days and we'll be there. How's Gina?"

Another beat of silence. "She's not doing well. I've confined her to her room for now. She's weak. I'm not sure she'll make it until you guys get back with the cure, but I'm doing everything I can to keep her alive."

Jace's throat bobbed. "Yeah, just … make her comfortable. We'll be back as fast as we can. Over."

No one said what we were all thinking, that unless we found a vehicle that could traverse the rough terrain at the next bunker, then it would be a several-day journey back to base.

"Stay safe. Over and out."

Jace tucked the radio back into his pack. "We should get some shut-eye."

Yes. I needed time to mull over the revelations of a few minutes ago, and my body ached for sleep. The sleeping bag was warm and cozy. The guys had all loved one woman. Not uncommon for a woman to be shared by a group of males in this new world, but what Jace described sounded safe and warm and perfect, and that wasn't how it always panned out. The women didn't usually get a choice. Julia had been one of the lucky ones, but she'd been ripped away from them by fate.

Logan's wariness, his animosity made sense now. Good to know it wasn't personal. My lips tingled with the memory of the kiss we'd shared in the hall of mirrors. He'd said I wasn't to his taste. Had he been making sure he wasn't attracted to me? Making sure they didn't fall into the same pattern they had with Julia?

No chance of that happening. I'd need to reassure him somehow. Long minutes ticked by, and Ash's even breathing, which usually lulled me to sleep, wasn't helping tonight. Fuck it, why was I still awake?

"I can't sleep either," Sage said softly from beside me.

I rolled onto my side to face the massive djinn. "I think my body is in overload mode."

Sage's eyes glowed like twin flames in the gloom. "Jace's revelations?"

"You heard?"

"I have excellent hearing."

"Yeah. It's a lot to process." I tucked an arm under my head.

"It's not the only thing you need to be pondering. What happened out there, Eva?"

I'd successfully pushed that question to the back of my thoughts. Funny, because I was usually all about the information and understanding how things worked, but there was a resistance in my mind, a block that urged me not to dwell too hard on what was happening inside me. It warned that delving would reveal something broken.

"You can't ignore it," Sage said softly. "Don't be the person that suspects they're sick but buries their head in the sand until it's too late."

Was that what I was doing? "Are you saying I'm sick?"

Sage pushed back the lip of his sleeping bag and reached down to grip the bottom of his T-shirt.

The pulse in my throat throbbed. "What are you doing?"

His smile was lopsided and knowing. "I need to show you something."

He slid his shirt up over his taut abs and flat pecs to reveal a softly glowing amber disc shape at his breastbone. It was the size of a golf ball.

"What is that?"

"I think that's my heart."

God, I wanted to touch it. "I don't understand."

"When djinn cross over to this plane, they leave behind their corporeal form, they leave behind their beating hearts." He paused as if searching for the words. "Scientifically speaking, we still have our hearts and form, but the frequency that this world exists on means that we don't have access to them like we would back home."

"So, you're forced to take hosts in order to affect this world."

"Yes, otherwise we are left to hover, watch, and whisper. There are other worlds where we have form. Worlds where we have power and humans live alongside us, but those worlds never interested me. Your world, however, with its fascinating dynamics and the fact we could hide and watch you like we were watching one of the reality shows humans loved so much, always appealed more to me."

"That's a little voyeuristic."

He grinned. "You have no idea. Djinn are inquisitive by nature, desperate to amass knowledge about the multiverse."

"Is that a thing?"

His smile was secretive. "You really do have no idea what wonders are out there. I've traveled, and I've seen so many worlds." His smile dropped. "I wasn't planning on getting stuck here. I never wanted to take a host, but circumstances gave me no choice. It's all very well being invisible when you can leave at any time, but not for eternity." He sighed. "I miss my home. The air heavy with jasmine and lavender, and the ability to summon fire whenever I want. But you ... You've changed that." He glanced down at his chest.

"This." My hand hovered above the amber disc on his breastbone, still desperate to touch it.

"This isn't supposed to be possible," Sage said. "Not on this plane, not with a human. Only a djinn can ignite another djinn's heart. It takes a special connection, a potential bond for it to happen, but never on this plane."

What was he saying? "What does this mean?"

"I'm not sure. But I think now I may be able to tap into my elemental ability without consequence." His gaze was warm on my face. "You did this, Eva. You gave this to me."

Special connection, a potential bond.

We barely knew each other. How could this be? He was hiding something. It was written all over his face. *Only a djinn can ignite another djinn's heart.*

"What aren't you telling me, Sage? You're not the only one that can read people. What's the significance of igniting another djinn's heart?"

His gaze was hooded. "Back in the djinn realm, when a djinn discovers a potential love match, their hearts ignite with an inner fire. It's like a mating call."

My breath hitched. "But I'm no djinn."

"Which is why it makes no sense," Sage said.

Okay, so I was focusing on the obvious issue, and not on the question of whether I was a potential match for him, because the latter was a gray area in my mind, one that was easily clouded by my body's reaction to him.

I allowed my fingers to graze the glowing spot on his chest. His skin was warm and velvet-soft beneath my hand. "I don't understand how I did this, or even if I really did do it."

"It was you. There is no other explanation. There's something about you, Eva. Something unique in your aura—threads of silver and gold, a miasma of color. It's beautiful."

"What do those colors mean?"

He shook his head. "I've seen thousands of auras in my long lifetime, but I've never seen one like yours before. It's truly unique."

The dark thought that had been circling my mind like a drain surged to the surface. I licked my lips, and he tracked the movement. "Am I human?"

He shuffled his sleeping bag closer and leaned in to press the tip of his nose to my forehead and inhaled. "You smell human, Eva. Sweet and filled with sunshine, but you *feel* as if you're more than human."

I tilted my head to meet his eyes. His mouth was so close that his honey breath teased my lips. "More?" My hand was still on his chest, palm flat now, and the spot heated beneath my touch.

Sage slid his hand across my jaw, threading his fingers into my hair and angling my head. "More."

His gravelly tone was delicious friction to my senses.

His attention was on my mouth, and mine dropped to his. Our breath mingled, my pulse fluttered then raced, and then he kissed me. A brush of his mouth over mine that sent tingles across my lips. He pulled back for a moment and returned to kiss my top lip, then the bottom one, before parting my mouth with the tip of his tongue and sweeping it across the seam of my lips as if asking permission. A soft moan climbed up my throat, and his fingers curled in my hair in response.

"Eva?" He said my name against my mouth.

He was holding back, just as he'd held back in the Wilds when I'd been under the remnants' spell. But I wasn't under a spell now. This was my choice, and every atom in my body wanted to taste him.

I wound my arms around his neck and kissed him hard. Even with the sleeping bags between us, even at the awkward angle, the shape of his mouth, the pressure of his lips, and the sweet burst of flavor from the rasp of his tongue felt right. The ache of nostalgia bloomed in my chest, as if this was what I'd been missing. Jasmine-scented air filled my lungs, marble etched with looping and intricate designs painted the insides of my eyelids. Sage's hand slipped from my hair to smooth down my front, over my breasts then up again to settle over my thudding heart.

He pulled back on the kiss, breaking contact with a series of soft pecks that teased and taunted me. I made a sound of protest, and his chest rumbled with the threat of laughter.

I pulled away. "You think it's funny to tease a lady?"

The corner of his mouth lifted as his gaze scanned my face. His grip on my hair tightened a split second before he claimed my mouth with tongue and teeth. He rolled on top of me, pinning me to the floor and kissing me so thoroughly my head began to reel.

This time, when he pulled back, his amber eyes were dark gold and swirling with flecks of silver. "Fucking hell, Eva. That will have to be enough, because if I don't stop, I'll have to take you right here, right now."

Something wicked reared its head inside my mind, and my hand, trapped between us, reached down to skim the hard bulge at his crotch. He hissed through his teeth, and then nipped my lip, following up with a flick of his tongue.

"Enough." He kissed me again. "Enough." He kissed me deeper this time. "Fuck." He rolled away, hand over his eyes. "Sleep. We can untangle the question of your abilities in the morning."

I snuggled down into the sleeping bag and closed my eyes, lips and body tingling from his attentions. Ash slept soundly to my right. Would it bother him that I'd kissed Sage? Did it bother me? It felt natural. Like it was meant to be. Like we were meant to be. Is this how Julia had felt with the Fangs? This longing for each of them, this ache in her soul. Once the world was no longer a fucked-up mess, maybe we'd be able to figure out what we all were to each other.

MY EYES POPPED OPEN, body wide awake. Something had changed. Something had woken me. The lamp was low; the batteries were probably almost out of juice. I strained to listen into the dark. How many hours had I slept? My eyes were still gritty, so not too long. I sat up slowly. Ash continued to slumber to my right, Sage snored softly to my left. Jace was curled up in his bag, and Logan …. Shit, where the fuck was Logan?

How long had he been gone?

A soft thud above us.

Logan?

Or had that noise woken the Fang? Had he gone to investigate? Idiot. Everyone knew you didn't go to investigate strange noises without backup. Pulling on my boots, I headed into the aisles.

"Logan? Logan?" I whisper-hissed.

Nothing.

If he was here, then he'd have heard me and answered. Shit. Back at our minicamp, I strapped on my sword and grabbed a flashlight before tapping Jace on the shoulder.

"Hmmm?" He opened a bleary eye to look up at me.

"Logan's gone off somewhere. I'm going to check on him. If we're not back in ten minutes, sound the alarm."

"Wha—"

But I was already headed for the exit, flashlight in hand, Talwar on my back, and a terrible foreboding blossoming in my stomach.

THE FOYER outside The Shack was littered with overturned metal bins and fake plants. The pitch-black darkness pressed in on me, and it took a moment for my eyes to adjust to the gloom surrounding the beam of my flashlight.

"Logan?"

My voice echoed in the silence.

Thud, scuffle. My head whipped up. Please let

that be him upstairs. We'd entered via the fire escape because the doors to the main stairs that led down here were blocked off. The lift lay open and dead. The only way up was through the fire doors. The beam of the flashlight bobbed across the dirty floor and over the fire exit. It bounded up the steps as I made my way stealthily to the ground floor. The door was smeared with brown and red and an awful smell hit my nostrils. Using the tip of my boot, I pushed the door open and ducked through onto the main floor of the service station.

Weak light filtered in through the many grimy windows, enough to see by. I flicked off the slender torch and tucked it into my back pocket. An old, dusty fountain sat in the foyer, surrounded by several wire baskets. A sweeping staircase sat beyond the fountain and a balcony ran around the perimeter at first-floor level. Shops glared at me like eyeless sockets, and a prickle ran up my spine.

I quashed the impulse to call out to Logan, listening to gut instinct. Walking on the balls of my feet and keeping to the pockets of heavy shadow, I headed left past two semi-shuttered shops, opening my senses, looking for any sign that Logan was here. Something dashed across the foyer in the periphery of my vision.

My body froze.

There, behind the fake potted plant. There was

something there. Not enough moonlight to see. My hand inched to the torch in my back pocket. Dammit. If I used the light, the thing, whatever it was, would know I'd spotted it. Could it see me?

Not Feral Fang, not Claw. Claws and Fangs didn't hide. They scented prey, and they attacked. This was something else.

Not Logan.

Definitely not Logan.

Another shadow ran along the balcony above, gone too soon. Shit. The one in the foyer had just moved again. It was behind the fountain now. A flash of ivory? Nails? Teeth.

My pulse was speeding up as adrenaline hit my system. The fire exit was mere meters away, but to get to it I'd need to head past the fountain, past the creature hiding there. Movement on the balcony. The thing was headed for the stairs. Shit. I glanced at the shop to my left — shutters almost all the way down, but enough space for someone of my size and stature to squeeze through. Wait, was that a bloody handprint? Glistening and still wet.

More movement, at the top of the stairs — a humanoid, hunched figure.

Fuck.

I leapt for the shutters, hit the ground, and rolled into the darkness beyond just as something slammed into the metal. A pale hand grabbed at me, fingers curled into claws. Not claws, nails. Human nails—long and thick and curled.

Oh, shit.

Human. The thing was human.

Another thud was followed by the shudder of the metal barrier. I needed to close it, wind it all the way closed. Usually the shutter doors would be controlled by an electrical panel, but there had to be a manual override. Using the torch and ignoring the growls and grunts from beyond, I located the panel on the wall by the doors. Beside it was a crank. Damn thing was stuck.

An arm pushed its way into the store all the way up to the shoulder. Hairless, pale skin mottled with inky black veins. Shit. If it persisted, could it force the shutter up? Two more arms slotted through.

Heart pulsing in my throat, I pushed on the crank.

Come on, Eva.

My neck strained, blood rushing in my ears as I pushed with all my might, and then, with a creak and a clatter, the shutter began to move. The things shrieked, and the arms vanished as the metal came down with a *clang*.

The darkness was now absolute. Shit, shit, shit. I had to get back down to the basement. I had to warn the others.

The flashlight beam scouted my surroundings to

find empty racks where clothes were once hung and toppled-over display stands. There had to be a back exit for fire purposes. Picking my way carefully over the debris, I headed to the back of the store. A low, purposeful growl had me pausing mid-step.

Seriously?

The coppery scent of blood hit me next, and then a shadow rushed at me. It swept me off my feet and cut off my yelp with a hand over my mouth, and then another aroma hit me, buried beneath the blood. Vanilla.

Logan?

He was moving fast but clumsily, and then we came to a halt. His chest rose and fell against my back, and his lips caressed my ear. "Shhh. There's something in here with us."

Chapter Eighteen

There's something in here with us . . .

Ice filtered through my veins in response to his words. I nodded beneath his hand, letting him know I got it, and he slowly uncovered my mouth and turned me in his arms. It was black as pitch, so impossible to see his face, but he was breathing too fast and shallow. Not good. I patted his chest, moving down until I hit the spot that made him hiss with pain, the spot that was wet, warm, and slick.

"How bad is it?" My pulse stalled. "Is it a bite?"

He gripped my hips, probably to steady himself. "No, it got me with its talons. I'm losing a lot of blood." His voice was barely above a whisper, and then his forehead pressed against mine, feverish hot. "It's fucking deep. It'll take time to heal; I need to stay still, but with that thing out there, just waiting, staying still isn't an option. I won't be able to stay conscious much longer if we don't patch up the wound."

Shit. "There are more of those things outside."

"Fucking great."

A lick of anger in my belly. "Why the hell did you come up here?"

"I heard a noise."

"Everyone knows you don't go investigate strange noises without backup. Have you never watched a slasher movie?"

"No."

Figured. He'd been an experiment, barely nine years old when he'd escaped into the awful wide world. No cinemas or movie nights for him. My hand was still on his chest, just above the wound, fingers grazing the rapid beat of his heart, and then he pulled away from my palm. It took a second to recognize the wobble, to realize he was keeling back. I made a grab for him in the dark and wrapped my arms around his waist to hold him steady. My face was level with his collarbones. It was the first time I'd been this close voluntarily, and it was like hugging a man carved from stone, all hard planes and dips.

"Eva ..." His mouth brushed my earlobe, sending a shiver through me.

There was no getting out of this without him. There was only one thing to do. "Drink." I tilted my head to the side, offering him my neck. "Quickly."

He inhaled sharply. "You sure?"

He wasn't turning me down, because he knew the predicament. He knew the only chance we had was if we were both in fighting form.

I swallowed the lump of apprehension in my throat. "Yeah, I'm sure. I need you."

His laugh was short and bitter. "No, you don't, but I'll take it." And then his fangs pierced my flesh. I pressed my mouth to his chest, gasping into the material, breath warm against the fabric of his shirt. His grip on me tightened as he drank from me, fingers pressing into my hips as if eager to leave impressions. I bit down on his shirt, on his flesh, to quell my moans as the euphoria rushed through my bloodstream like a delicious heat wave. My hips jerked in primal reaction to the pleasure that he was injecting into me. Oh, God. Please be over. Even as the thought swam through my mind, I was holding him tighter, urging him to continue, to take more, to give more.

His chest rumbled, and then he pulled back, mouth still brushing my neck but fangs no longer piercing it. The silence was interrupted by our ragged breath and the sharp tang of pheromones.

His hands skimmed up my spine, fingers moving as if he was playing a tune.

"Logan." My voice cracked.

"I'm done." He laved my neck to close the wound.

If it was over, then why was my body still singing? Why was I still holding onto him as if he were a life raft? Why was my mouth traveling up to caress the base of his throat?

The muscles beneath my hands tensed, and he sucked air in through his teeth. "Dammit, Eva. Snap out of it. So not the time." His voice was harsh, almost angry.

I dropped my chin, reining in the rolling desire. Fuck. This wasn't me.

My head cleared. "Good. I'm good. You?"

"Healed up. Now let's get the fuck out of here."

We needed to take stock of the situation. "There's one in the store and two outside. I think they're human."

"I know."

"How is this possible?"

"I can't answer that, so let's focus on staying alive long enough to figure it out."

"I can't see a damn thing. I'm useless in a fight right now."

"I don't think that thing can see too well either, but I can see it fine. It's camped out toward the rear of the store. I don't know if it realizes there's an exit only a meter away, and I'd rather it doesn't find out."

A plan formed in my mind. "We can use my flashlight to distract it, draw it away from the exit. I'll act as bait, and then you can take it out. Once it's down, we take the rear exit, grab the others, and get the fuck out of here."

"Sounds good."

I made to take a step back, but he cupped my shoulders, holding me in place. "Why'd you come after me, Eva?"

What? "I woke up, and you were gone. I was worried."

"So, you came after me without backup?" There was a smile in his voice, a hint of the cocky Fang I knew he could be.

"I woke Jace and told him … Oh, fuck."

"What?"

"I told Jace that if I wasn't back in ten minutes he should sound the alarm."

"Dammit."

It had been more than ten minutes. No doubt Ash and Jace or Sage would be coming to look for me and Logan. Shit.

"We need to get back out there, Logan. If they come up those stairs, they'll be walking into an ambush."

There was no time to waste. My flashlight bloomed to life; the room lit up, and Logan's beautiful face was finally visible. His perfect mouth was a determined line, lips rosy from feeding. We were in a small changing room. I swung the beam of light, found the door, and headed out onto the shop floor.

"Come out, come out wherever you are." My tone was a taunt.

The light swept the floor before snagging on the pale form headed right for me. I turned and ran, hopefully in the right direction. Metal clinked and scraped across the ground as the thing pursued, my blood rushed in my ears, and the flashlight beam dashed about like crazy. Metal shutters. Yes!

A yelp and a growl were followed by a snarl that was pure Logan. I spun, locating them with my light. Logan was in full Claw mode with the pale Feral human pinned beneath him. The human was naked and hairless, its eye whites crimson and glaring, and its mouth was an aperture filled with jagged teeth that snapped desperately, trying to take a bite out of Logan. And then Logan ripped its head off with a slash of his claws.

I stood, back to the shutters, heart hammering to get out of my chest as if I'd run a marathon — running from a monster would do that to a girl. Logan rose off the Feral and padded toward me. His dark fur rippled with the pantherine movement of his body, and fear tightened my abdomen. This was Logan. He wouldn't hurt me. He came to a standstill before me, his snout barely a foot away from me. Damn, he was big in this form, his head coming up to my collarbone. My hand reached out as if of its own volition and stroked him, running from between his eyes to down his nose. He was silken and smooth and so fucking powerful. He chuffed and shook his head.

Something slammed into the shutters behind us. I jerked in surprise, and Logan snarled low in his throat.

An exclamation followed in a voice I recognized.

Sage.

I rushed to the shutter controls. "We have to get out there."

The crank wasn't so stiff this time, but it was still a bitch to turn. And then Logan was at my back in his Fang form. His hands cupped mine, helping to wind the shutters up halfway. Enough for us to duck into the moonlit foyer to join Sage and Ash.

Sage was lit up, his hands balls of flame. Two Feral lay dead on the ground by the fountain. Heads twisted at odd angles. Ash's work, no doubt. The rest hovered at the foot of the stairs, held at bay by the threat of fire. They were tall and short and squat and slender. The varied shapes and sizes that humans came in, and they were naked and hairless. Feral humans ... How the fuck?

"If I light them up, this whole place will go up in flames," Sage said softly so as not to spook the monsters. "They're not going to stay back for much longer, though."

Ash's crossbow was strapped to his back—no good in close quarters, and getting up close to snap heads was risking a bite, risking infection. Logan's bat was nowhere to be seen. He must have dropped it in the store, but they could both shift to wolf form. In wolf form, they could use their claws, and their hides were too thick for the Feral to bite through. In wolf form, they were safer from infection because any blood they did accidentally ingest when tearing off Feral limbs would be filtered out of their systems before hitting their bloodstream.

I looked to Sage, but his attention was on the threat. "Sage, on the count of three, I want you to make a run for the fire exit. Get Jace and Benji and get out of here. Head north. We'll catch up."

"Like hell am I leaving you." His gravelly voice was deeper than usual.

I drew my sword. "I'll be fine. I have Ash and Logan. We'll take care of the Feral and join you shortly."

He looked torn, but then he nodded. His muscles rippled as he prepared to make a dash.

"One. Two. Three."

Sage turned and ran. For a split second, the Feral did nothing, and then they surged toward us. Motorhead blared in my head, and my sword cut a path through the air, ready for the dance.

THE FERAL HUMANS were strong and fast. Almost as strong and fast as the Feral Fang, but not quite. My sword cut through flesh and sinew, and the guys mauled and maimed with fang and claw.

It took mere minutes, and then we were standing in the midst of a bloodbath. My borrowed oversized clothes were spattered with blood, and my sword was kissed with crimson.

"More will come," Logan said. "Ash can hear heartbeats, erratic and getting closer. There are more above us."

"Let's get out of here before they come down."

I turned and ran with them, back through the fire doors and out into the night. The others would have been away by now. Please let them have made it out.

"There!" Logan said.

Two figures were up ahead, sprinting farther and farther away. Sage and Jace had made it out. Thank goodness. The land before us was bordered by woodland. It had once been a slip road and was now home to nature.

"Twenty miles to our next stop," Logan said. "Doesn't look like we'll be getting much rest."

Our next stop—the Claw camp that Noah had told us about. To seek refuge with his friend Nate Summers before making our way to the second bunker. Twenty miles … my feet ached at the thought.

Up ahead, the two figures had slowed down, wait … what was happening? "They're headed back this way."

Logan and Ash slowed down and came to a standstill. "What's that behind them?"

Shadows poured out of the woodland, pale in the moonlight. Feral humans. A sob caught in my throat, not fear but frustration. How much more? Seriously? What the fuck?

I drew my sword and broke into a sprint toward the guys. Up ahead, Jace's body blurred, shifting into his silver wolf form. Sage faltered and Jace snapped at him, as if to say *go*, before turning back toward the Feral.

Almost there.

"No!" Benji screamed as Sage put him down. Fire lit up the night, hitting the Feral and setting them alight.

"Watch out!" Logan shouted. "You'll set the woods alight."

Benji's terrified face glared up at me as I passed him. I swerved to the right, running parallel to the fire to cut off another wave of Feral humans. The Talwar opened throats in a neat, orderly line.

"Too many," Sage called out. "There's too many."

My heart sank, because he was right. The woods were crawling with them, and the fire was drawing them to us, as some primitive part of what was left of their brains probably associating it with safety and home brought them out from hiding.

Ash's golden flank was to my left, snapping and snarling to keep the Feral off me. Logan's chestnut body growled to my right. This time, it wouldn't be enough.

"Fall back." I began to walk backwards, away from the infested woods. "We need to make a run for it."

"Nowhere to run," Sage said. "They're coming out of the service station."

Sure enough, figures were clambering up the rise toward us from the building. We were food, they were hungry, and we were pinned in with nowhere to run.

I met Sage's eyes briefly as he cradled the boy in his arm. The rage and sorrow swirling in their golden depths mingled with the dark despair opening like a chasm inside me.

I'd been trained not to give up, to find an opportunity in every situation, to survive at all costs, and Dad's voice had always been there to advise and urge me on. But for the first time since he'd gone, there was only silence in my head.

A silence that shouted out that we were fucked.

But I'd be damned if I'd go down without a fight. If those fuckers wanted to feast, they'd have to get past my blade. My sword played its tune, and my body danced, taking out as many Feral as it could. The Fangs did the same. Keep fighting, just keep —

The roar of an engine rose over the crackle of fire and the rush of blood in my head. Headlights blinded me, and then a beast of a vehicle slammed into the horde, flattening the Feral in its wake before coming to a grinding halt across the path, engine idling.

It was an armored van, customized for rough terrain with Tonka truck wheels, bars at the windows, and spikes on the boot and hood. The side door slid open, and a pixie-haired woman dangled out.

"Get the fuck in if you want to live."

There was no time to hesitate. The van meant life. Sage handed Benji over, and then helped me up into the vehicle before climbing in. Seats lined the opposite wall, and I fell onto one as Jace, Ash, and Logan filled the space behind me. Benji climbed onto my lap. The door slammed shut and we were off, bumping and jolting as we left the monsters behind.

The woman opened a hatch to the driver's section. "Take the short route."

"You got it, Kira."

She shut the hatch, turned to us, and grabbed a handhold built into the roof of the van. Feet planted shoulder-width apart, she managed to stay upright and stable as the van made some nifty turns. If not for Ash on one side and Sage on the other, I'd have fallen off my seat.

"You Noah's boys?" she said.

"Yes," Logan said. "Please tell me you're Nate's people."

She grinned, showcasing even white teeth. "We're Nate's people. Picked up a call from Noah about an hour ago on our satcom. Told us you were holed up here and would be with us tomorrow before sunset. Nate remembered this place was infested so sent us to get you."

And thank God he had. Thank God Noah had called in. "Thank you. You saved our lives."

She smirked. "You looked like you were handling yourself pretty well."

"Would have flagged eventually under the onslaught. Those fuckers don't tire."

Her expression sobered. "No, they don't."

"Human Feral ... how long?"

"A few months." She cocked her head as if listening to something. "We'll hit smooth terrain in a moment. Relax, you're safe. We'll be at camp in about half an hour."

Benji whimpered in my arms, and Kira's gaze dropped to the child; her nose twitched and then her face softened. "He's one of us."

I nodded. "His mother didn't make it."

She sighed. "They were on the way to us?"

"Yes."

"In that case, he'll be well looked after. Thank you for saving him."

I leaned my cheek on the top of Benji's head and closed my eyes. Almost there, we were almost there.

Chapter Nineteen

ELIAS

The Wilds, the fucking Wilds. They'd taken a shortcut. Fools. I'd never been into the Wilds myself, but Malcolm had sent scouts; not all had returned, and the tales the survivors had spouted had filled my blood with ice.

Fools.

The terrain was rough, and the bike was suffering now; I'd have to get on foot soon. No choice on that. I'd been lucky it had lasted this long. Common sense dictated that if they'd cut through the Wilds they'd have exited onto a road called the A6, which led to Kirkstone Pass, but the landscape was no longer the same as the old maps. Overgrown and unkempt, the signs that had once populated the Island were hidden from view. But if that was where they were headed, then I was on the right road to finding them. A building rose up to my left, gray and imposing on a backdrop of orange and red.

Fire.

Fire was man-made, which meant humans, or maybe it was her. I swerved the bike onto the slip road, headed in the direction of the flames. Figures battled up ahead. The flash of a sword and the snarl of wolves.

It was her. It had to be, and she was in danger. I revved the engine of the bike, and a roar ripped the air as another engine drowned out the sound of my bike. A moment later, an armored vehicle crushed through the woods, taking out the Feral. The figures on the ground didn't hesitate to pile in.

Safe. She was safe.

The van pulled away, hurtling back into the woods. I revved my engine and followed. I had her, and I wasn't letting her out of my sight.

Chapter Twenty

The Claw camp was located in a huge clearing in the dense forests on the outskirts of what had once been the county of Derbyshire. This site had once been a national park but was now an overgrown wilderness. The perimeter was fortified with fences made of chopped-down tree trunks, electrified barbed wire running off generators, and huge, hulking sentries. Fire sconces lit the perimeter, pushing back the shadows. Figures walked about between huge teepee tents or sat around roaring camp fires chatting, amiable and relaxed. The aroma of roasting meat filled the air, and my stomach cramped in hunger. How long had it been since I'd had a proper hot, meaty meal?

Too long.

We followed Kira and what seemed to be her second in command past a set of sentries and into the camp proper. Benji held tight to my hand, walking close.

A woman approached, faltering a few feet away. She shook her head in confusion.

"What's wrong, Lana?" Kira asked.

"I thought … I thought I smelled someone." She laughed nervously. "My sister, Mika."

"Mummy's name was Mika," Benji said in a small voice.

Lana's hand went to her mouth. "Oh. Oh, hello …" Her gaze flicked up to Kira.

Kira nodded. "His mother was on her way here with him. I'm sorry, Lana, she didn't make it."

Lana pressed her lips together, her eyes misting. "Okay. Right." She walked closer and crouched a few feet away, her attention on Benji. "Hi. I think … I think I'm your aunt."

"I'm Benji," Benji said. He held up his bear. "This is Pookie." He sniffed.

"Wow, can I see?"

Benji looked up at me. I nodded and let go of his hand. He stood, uncertain for a moment, and then walked over to Lana to show her the bear. It was obvious in her expression, in the tension in her body that she was aching to hug the boy, but she held back, not wanting to spook him.

"It's a lovely bear. You know, I have a daughter, your cousin, she's around the same age as you, and I know she'd love to meet you and Pookie. I think your mummy was coming here to find me, Benji. I …" Her voice cracked. "I'd like to take care of you if you'd let me."

Benji looked over his shoulder at me again, and once again I nodded.

"Okay," he said to Lana.

She offered him her hand, and he took it. "Thank you," she said to us. "Thank you so much for keeping him safe."

Fuck, now I was getting teary. "You're welcome."

Kira blew out a breath. "Well, that worked out well. We should get you guys to HQ."

Another hit of fragrant food assaulted my senses.

"Man, that smells good." Jace rubbed his stomach.

"Crap, of course, you guys must be starving," Kira said. "Tell you what? Carter will get you some food, and once you've fueled up, he'll bring you over to HQ." She strode off and vanished between two blue tents.

Carter, a slender young man with wide swimmer's shoulders, shot us a reassuring smile. "We have deer tonight, freshly caught. I think Dima may even have rustled up some bread."

My mouth watered as we made our way through the camp, drawing curious gazes that glittered in the firelight. This was a camp of uninfected Claws, creatures that had banded together and managed to avoid death. Creatures that looked all too human in their non-furry forms, albeit large, muscular humans.

"It's an impressive setup," Sage said to Carter conversationally. "I don't sense any wards, though."

"That's because we don't have any. If any Feral do make it this far, we take care of them. There are traps all around the camp. Traps only we know the location of. Feral aren't the smartest creatures." We came to a stop at a pretty purple gazebo-style tent that had been customized into a kitchen space. Pots bubbled over spitting flames, and a woman chopped vegetables at a long, wide oak table surrounded by several chairs. She wiped her hands on her apron and jerked her chin up in greeting as we approached. Like most Claw females, she was powerfully built, tall with arms corded with muscle, but her face was a delicate oval with slanted eyes and thick lashes.

"These Noah's boys?"

"They are indeed."

Her eyes lit up. "Good man, Noah." Her gaze skimmed over Ash, Logan, and Jace. "You probably don't remember me, do you?"

Jace's face softened as if summoning a memory. "You made sweets for us."

She grinned. "That's right. I did."

Logan snapped his fingers. "Pastry. I remember the pastry with jam inside."

Her grin widened, and her attention fell to Ash. "And you loved my stew. Would eat bowls of it. And look at you now, strapping lad."

Ash smiled with his eyes.

Her gaze raked over Sage and her mouth turned up slightly at the corners. "And who are you?"

"Name's Sage." The big djinn gave her his most charming smile, the one that flipped my stomach when it had been aimed at me.

"A djinn. Nice." There was a definite suggestion to her tone, a purring quality that was almost sexual.

My stomach tightened, and I instinctively stepped closer to Sage.

Her gaze flicked to me, and she arched a brow. "Human …" She frowned. "You smell odd."

"Gee, thanks. You try running from all kinds of monsters for two days and see how flowery you smell."

She snorted. "I think we can help you with that problem. But I assume you want feeding first?"

My stomach grumbled way too loud, and she let out a bark of laughter. "I love a woman with an appetite."

"You love women full stop," Carter said.

Oh. Right.

"And men," the Claw said. "I don't discriminate."

She waved us over to the table. "The name's Dima. Grab a seat, and we'll get you fueled up."

Chairs scraped as we took places at the huge table, and then fragrant earthen bowls of a meaty concoction were set before us. Flatbread was placed within reach, and that was it, I was off, digging in as if my life depended on it. Hunger gnawed at my insides, violent and ferocious as if smacked awake by the prospect of a real meal. My bowl was empty too fast, but it was refilled just as quickly and emptied once more.

I was the first to start and the last to finish.

Ash placed a hand on my thigh, his fingers warm through the fabric of my borrowed bloody joggers. I covered the top of his hand with mine.

"You must have a hell of a metabolism," Dima said.

I shrugged. "This was delicious."

I got up to help clear away the dishes, and the guys stood with me, gathering bowls and passing them to Carter, who put them into a wooden trough filled with water.

"How is Noah?" Dima asked. "It's been a long time."

"He's good," Logan said.

She arched a brow. "No ... *episodes*?"

She knew about those?

Logan was silent.

Dima sighed. "Nate asked him to stay with us, thought we may be able to help, and you boys ... we wanted you to be a part of our pack. But he's a stubborn man. He believed there were answers out there. A reason, a purpose for your existence aside from the obvious experimentation. I'm not sure what he hoped to find."

"We've been good," Jace said. "Noah's been doing good."

Dima glanced across at Carter. "You want to go grab some fresh water from the well?"

Carter frowned but got up, grabbed another bucket, and headed off. Dima watched him go and then leaned in.

"Is there really a cure?" she asked.

She knew? Noah must have told Nate. "How many Claws know?"

She shook her head. "Just Nate, me, and Kira so far. I can't believe it."

"It's true," Logan said.

She nodded. "I believe you."

Because he couldn't lie? "We'll know more in a few days."

"How far have you left to travel?"

"Another four hundred miles," Jace said. "Maybe more, I'd have to check the map and replot our course."

"Four hundred miles can be achieved in a day."

"Not on foot, they can't," Sage said.

"You're on foot?" Her brows shot up. "You may have survived on foot this far but you won't make it on foot if you're headed north."

"Why?" Sage asked.

"If you think the service station they plucked you from is bad you've seen nothing. The further north you go, the worse it gets. It's infested with human Feral." Her eyes darkened. "They're every-where, and they're slowly moving south."

"The virus must have mutated," Jace said, tugging gently on his bottom lip. I'd noticed he did this when he was unraveling a thought. "Or it could be a secondary effect of the virus, a dormant feature that has now been activated." He looked up. "We'd need to capture a human Feral to find out for sure."

"Or we could just focus on getting the cure," Logan said sarcastically.

But my scalp was prickling with a revelation that had my heart sinking. "But if the cure was designed for the original virus, will it even work on the mutated form?"

Jace shook his head. "Probably not, but with the building blocks, we could engineer a new cure, one for the existing virus and one for the mutated version. Slight modifications and a sample of blood from a Feral human would be enough to get to work on the problem."

And the Genesis lab we were headed for should have that equipment. "We can do this."

"Not on foot you can't," Dima reminded us. "Let me speak to Nate. I think I may have a solution."

Carter returned with the water, and Dima fetched some cups. "Drink up and then we'll head over to HQ."

HQ WAS like a miniature circus tent. Sentries sat around a large crate outside the entrance, engrossed in a game of cards with a lone lamp for light. They looked up and waved at Dima as she sashayed past with us in tow. Carter didn't follow us into the tent; instead he grabbed a chair and joined the guys in their card game.

The inside of the tent was warm and cozy. Furs and cushions lined the floors and lamps lit the space. A round table sat in the center, and a large silver-haired man draped in furs held court. Kira and two other Claws were at the table with the man who had to be Nate, the pack alpha. Dima took the seat beside him.

His piercing green eyes assessed us as we walked over. I met his gaze levelly and his mouth tightened slightly. Was it bad etiquette to stare an alpha in the eyes? Fuck it, I wasn't a Claw, and I wasn't pack.

"We don't usually entertain humans," he said to me. "But Noah was insistent that you were important. You have the key."

"I do."

"Show it to me."

Demanding much? I tugged the key from under my oversized jumper and held it up. "There you go."

He made a give-it-here gesture, but I tucked the key back under my jumper. "No."

He arched a blond brow. "No?"

Kira tensed.

I held up my hands. "Look, you're the alpha here, I get that, but I'm not a Claw, and you're not my alpha, so please don't look so shocked when I don't jump when you demand it."

There was a long beat of silence, and then he leaned back in his seat, picked up his mug, and took a drink.

Kira visibly relaxed.

"Come join us," Nate said. "If you wouldn't mind?"

He was mocking me, but that was okay. "Thank you."

I took a seat at the table, and Logan and Ash pulled out the seats either side of me, framing me with their reassuring bulks. Sage remained standing, and Jace took the seat beside Kira. She shot him a smile, and his cheeks flushed.

"If this is real," Nate said, "then it could change everything."

He was preaching to the choir. "I know."

"The Vladul have the upper hand right now. They have power over the Feral Fangs, they have the Genesis Foundation and all the technology, and they're creating goodness knows what inside their labs. This could save us. If we can cure the infected Claws, we can swell our numbers and bring the Vladul down."

It didn't escape my notice that he'd only mentioned the Claws. "Not just the Claws. We'll cure the Fangs too, and any humans who may be infected."

His lips tightened. "Yes. Well, of course. But we should cure the Claws first."

Of course? Ha. He was thinking about his own people. He was thinking strategically—Claw numbers over Feral Fang numbers, but my strategy was better.

"Really? I would have thought the priority would be to cure the Feral Fangs and take away the

Vladul advantage. No Feral to control would surely be a blow to their plans."

Nate was studying me with a new light in his eyes. "Yes. I suppose it would."

Sage sighed heavily. "Eva, remember how I wanted to kill Ash, Logan, and Jace when we crossed paths?"

"Um, yes …" Why was he bringing this up now?

"It's because the Vladul have ways to control uninfected Fangs. A year ago, a group of Fangs we traded with, a group that hated the Vladul, were taken by Vladul soldiers. The same Fangs attacked our camp a month later. We fought them off, and I even captured one of them, and I swear, when I looked in his eyes, there was nothing. It was as if he didn't even remember who I was. The Vladul had done something to them, reprogrammed them somehow. We moved camp after that and started hunting Fangs. I would have killed Jace, Logan, and Ash if they were pure Fang."

Nate's smile was wicked. "So, we cure the Claws first. Take down the Vladul, then cure the Feral Fangs."

Fuck. I inclined my head. "It seems the best way forward in light of the new information."

Dima picked up her mug and took a dainty sip. "They're planning on heading north on foot, Nate," she said. "They'll never make it."

"You want me to send an escort."

She set her mug on the table. "If you feel it's best."

Nate was silent for a long time. "I do. Which is why I've already charged Kira to take a team and accompany them. They'll take the armored van and leave at dawn."

Every muscle in my body unknotted. No more walking, no more fighting. "Thank you."

He inclined his head. "On one condition."

Of course there'd be a condition. "Name it."

"You come straight back here with the cure first."

Dima shifted uncomfortably in her seat, refusing to meet my gaze. She was hiding something.

"We have no idea what form the cure will be in," Jace pointed out. "It may be a formula, it may be a vaccine, and we may have to synthesize more."

"Then you do what you have to and bring some of that vaccine here first," Nate said evenly.

"And if, by some fluke, the lab the cure is held at doesn't have the equipment we need?" Jace asked. He forged on, not waiting for a response. "We'd have to go back to base to use the limited equipment there."

Nate rubbed his chin. "I see. In that case, we would take you back to your base and wait with you until you've synthesized enough of the vaccine. Enough to send back here."

I didn't get it. "Why do you want the vaccine so bad? No one here is infected."

He frowned. "Maybe not, but the forest to the east of here is filled with infected Feral Claws, Claws that were once part of this united pack. I won't let them suffer any longer than needed. I don't believe it's asking much. The rest of the cure can be distributed how you wish."

"United pack?" Sage asked. "As in, the only pack?"

Nate inclined his head. "That's right. This is all that is left of the Claws. Once, there were five packs, five alphas, and now there is only one alpha and one pack. We take in whoever survives and makes it here."

There couldn't be more than maybe a hundred Claws in this camp. They were going extinct. If there was a way to stop that, then I couldn't stand in the way.

"You have a deal. We'll make sure you get the first batch of the cure."

Nate nodded curtly. "I'm surprised Noah allowed you to make this journey on foot in the first place."

"We had a van," Jace said, glancing at Sage.

"But it wouldn't have made the trip. We had to leave it part way through our journey."

Nate locked gazes with me. "The armored van will ensure your safety. I'm no fool, Eva. The key is tied to you. That much is clear. If your father had something to do with the cure, then he would have security measures in place to ensure only the person he entrusted the key to would be able to unlock it. Noah and I both believe there is no access to the cure without you."

I stared at him, this large man draped in fur, this imposing figure with a hard-set jaw and eyes filled with sorrow.

"In that case, we'll leave at first light."

Chapter Twenty-One

ELIAS

A Claw camp? Dammit. There was no way in without being noticed, but my gut told me this was my last chance to get to her. Best to scout the perimeter, steering clear of the traps. Traps that weren't hidden too well. Obviously meant to deter Feral, not Vladul. Traps were another of my skill sets. Tracking, trapping, hunting. It was in my blood. Royal blood from a time when we'd hidden behind castles made of mortar in tiny villages populated by unsuspecting humans eager to please their landlords. We'd supped on blood, leaving our victims alive. It had been the royal way until Malcolm and his uprising had ruined it for us, dragging us into the light and forcing us to run and hide. His ilk that believed they, the predator, deserved to hunt and kill unchecked. That humans were merely cattle to be consumed and bred.

No care for their sensibilities. No care for their pain. Mother, our queen, our leader ... if she could see the Vladul now ... If she could see what her usurper was trying to achieve. I needed to stop him, for her, to preserve her legacy and restore us to the creatures we once had been. Not monsters. Not evil. But protectors of humanity linked by blood in a symbiotic relationship. The key would do that. It would give me control of our new empire and allow me to liberate my people.

But what if the woman carrying the key fought? What if she refused to give it up?

The thought of having to hurt her made my stomach turn, but it would be one life to save the many.

My feet avoided branches and crispy bracken, sticking to the softer earth. Yes, I was leaving prints, but by the time those were discovered I'd be long gone with my prize. There had to be some weakness, a place where I could breach their defenses. But the thick fence and the electrified wire extended throughout.

A moment, I needed a—what was that? That scent?

Feral ... not Fang. Claws.

The wind was in my favor, bringing their scent

to me but keeping my scent away from them. My boots made not a sound as I wove through the trees. Snarls and growls grew louder and metal glinted in the moonlight. I padded closer. Several large cages stood stationed side by side, and inside, pacing and frothing, red-eyed and hungry, were several Feral Claws.

This was it. This was the perfect plan.

I stepped into the moonlight, facing the cages. "How would you like to go for a run?"

Chapter Twenty-Two

The Claws had provided us with a tent and a couple of buckets of water from the well to get cleaned up. Kira had even provided me with a change of clothes. Hers, no doubt—pants made of soft leather and a long-sleeved top. Both black. The guys had wandered off, leaving me to wash and change in our tent. The temperature was dropping and so I hurried to wash and get into the clean clothes, and damn, did it feel good to be fresh.

"Knock, knock," Sage said from outside.

"I'm decent, you can come in."

"Shame." He ducked under the flap, his eyes like embers lighting the gloom. "You look good in that." He raked me over. "It suits you."

I plucked at the shirt. "A little big."

He shrugged. "Claw females are larger than humans." He canted his head in thought. "So are djinn females." His eyes lit up. "And Fang females."

"I get it. I'm a Barbie doll."

"No, Eva. You're no Barbie doll. You're a force of nature." His voice had deepened into that extra gravelly tone that rubbed against my senses in delicious friction.

A shiver ripped through me. It was the chill, nothing else.

"You're cold," Sage said.

"Yeah, the temperature has dropped."

He frowned. "No, it hasn't."

I climbed onto the pile of furs that made up the makeshift bed. "How would you know? You're made of smokeless fire."

He eyed the piles of fur. "I am pretty hot. Would you like me to sleep beside you?"

Shit, he was getting closer, his presence sucking the oxygen from the room, like the creature of fire he was.

"Sure."

One corner of his mouth lifted, and he lowered himself onto the bed. His arm brushed mine, deliciously warm. I sighed and shifted closer, rolling onto my side to bask in his heat. He stared at the ceiling of the tent.

My fingers ached to reach out and trace the smooth lines of his profile, granite and chiseled.

He sighed. "This time tomorrow, we'll have the cure. This time tomorrow, we'll have answers. We'll know what it is we're dealing with. And then we'll have to part ways."

A stabbing pain in my chest. "What do you mean?"

"I have a camp to get back to, Eva. Responsibilities. My people are waiting for results. I'll need to go back and reassure them and rally them to help spread the cure. I'll need to organize our mission to get into Genesis in preparation for our attack. My people are still being held hostage by the Vladul."

"And so is my friend, along with many humans. We'll storm the gates together. Once we've dispatched the cure, we'll build an army of Claws and Fang and djinn, and we'll force the Vladul out of their stronghold." I'd shifted closer, heart racing with determination. "We can do this, Sage, but I need you by my side."

Maybe need was the wrong word. Scratch that, it was definitely the wrong word. I didn't need him, I wanted him. His big bad presence, his fiery gaze, his humor, and the way he could cut right through my bullshit. Whereas Ash was an anchor to steady me, Sage was a reality check that grounded my emotions. Maybe I did need him after all?

He rolled onto his side so his breath mingled with mine. "If you want me to stay, Eva, all you have to do is ask." His lips hovered over mine. "Make a wish."

"A wish?"

"Yes."

My gaze fell to his mouth. "I wish you'd kiss me."

"Granted." His voice was a growl.

And then his mouth crushed mine. His hand slid into the hair at the base of my scalp to angle my head and deepen the kiss, stealing my breath and flipping my stomach with the sudden intensity. His touch incited a fever in me that momentarily chased away the chill. He pulled away too soon, and a sound of protest tripped from my lips.

His chest rumbled in a chuckle. "No more. Not now, not here. I may be a voyeur, but I don't like an audience."

Audience? Ash's cinnamon scent hit me then. I sat up as he ducked into the tent. His pale gaze raked over us, entwined on the bed, and then he kicked off his shoes and dropped onto the furs on the other side of me.

"Eva was feeling cold." Sage's tone was conversational.

Ash slung an arm around my waist and pressed

his chest to my back. His body heat seeped through my clothes.

"Better?" Sage asked.

"Much better."

Ash nuzzled my neck, his tongue flicking out to taste me. The juncture at my thighs throbbed in response, and I squeezed my legs together as heat bloomed low in my belly.

Sage tutted. "I wouldn't start something you can't finish, Ash. Hardly fair on the lady, don't you think?"

Ash raised his head and sighed before settling behind me, his palm splayed across my stomach.

What was this?

Sage smiled down at me. "Ash and I have an understanding."

"You do?" I looked over my shoulder at Ash. "What kind of understanding?"

Ash looked across at Sage as if prompting him to answer.

"We understand that we both have feelings for you," Sage said. "And that we both want to be with you. We understand that we want you to be happy, and we understand that a woman like you doesn't come along every day, that these feelings don't manifest easily for us. We understand that there will be boundaries and respect and possibly, sometime in the future, a timetable for your attentions."

A sharp bark of surprised laughter spilled from my lips. "A schedule?"

He arched a brow. "Unless you want us at the same time."

Ash growled.

Sage's grin was filled with mischief. "Fine, so Ash isn't down for that."

"You guys seem to have this all figured out."

His expression grew serious. "Whatever you need, Eva. The world has changed and with it so has the shape of love."

Ash kissed the nape of my neck, but it was less sexual and more reassuring.

Could this really happen? Could we do this? I wanted them both, there was no doubt about that, and a future without them made my chest ache with a yawning emptiness. Strange when until a week ago I'd been a sole survivor, prepared to go it alone, prepared to have no attachment, no ties. These males had changed me. They'd burrowed into my soul, into the heart of me where the true Eva hid, the one who longed to connect. The one who wanted more than mere survival. The one who wanted to live.

Tobias's face came to mind, his emerald gaze always so warm and filled with compassion and understanding. Would he be able to love me like this? Because I knew in that moment, without a shadow of a doubt, that I couldn't give up the possibility of Ash or Sage.

I snuggled back into Ash and tugged Sage closer. "Thank you."

"Cozy." Logan's sarcastic tone filled the room.

My body tensed. Damn him and his bucket of ice-cold water attitude. "Yeah, it is, actually." I raised both brows. "Care to join?"

Shit, where had that come from.

He snorted. "No, thanks. Not for me."

"Watch your tone, Logan," Sage said. There was steel in his tone, something I hadn't heard before.

"Why?" Logan said. "So you can play happy families and forget that she's human? You're begging for heartache. Human lives are fleeting and fragile and good for only one thing. Blood. And with the shit we're going to have to deal with, hers could be more fleeting than others."

Ash was on his feet and in Logan's face in a blink, but Logan didn't back down this time; instead he lifted his chin and stood his ground.

"What? You gonna hit me for telling the truth, for saying what we're all thinking? There's a war on the horizon. One where we're going to have to fight the most powerful fucking supernaturals in the history of forever. Maybe we'll have a cure, and maybe we'll have the numbers, but the focus will have to be on the fight. It can't be on anything else, especially not the safety of one human woman."

I sat up. "I can take care of myself. Have been doing so for years. In fact, I recall I saved your arse back at the service station."

"Your blood saved my life, Eva. Not you. Just blood. Don't get it twisted." His dark eyes flashed with venom that pierced my soul.

My ears burned with embarrassed anger. "I'm not Julia, and shit doesn't have to repeat itself."

Ash's back rippled with tension and Logan's face contorted into something between fury and agony.

"Jace, that fucking little —"

"What?" Jace entered the tent.

Logan turned on him. "You told her. You fucking told her about Julia."

Jace's face drained of color, but he stood tall, shoulders pushed back. "She needed to know. She needed to understand why you were being such an arsehole."

Logan shook his head. "You had no right. None." He stormed out of the tent.

Jace's shoulders slumped.

Oh, shit, me and my big mouth. "I'm sorry, Jace."

"It's not your fault. He needs to let it go. We can't stop loving just because we may lose the person we love. It's no way to live. Especially not in a world where love is the only thing that could alle-viate the horror."

Ash placed a hand on Jace's shoulder.

"Should we go after Logan?" Sage asked.

"No," Jace said. "He'll be back. He just needs time to cool off."

Ash walked back to the bed and lay down, but Jace hovered in the doorway.

I patted the furs. "There's plenty of room."

He looked torn for a moment, and then tugged off his boots and joined us on the pile of furs on the other side of Sage.

"Feel free to snuggle," Sage said.

Jace snort-laughed. "Thanks, mate. I think I'll pass."

Somewhere between worrying about having hurt Logan and soaking in the heat thrown off by the guys, sleep stole over me like a sneaky bitch. And then I was running through the forest, dark green leaves slapping at my face, moist earth beneath my boots. Snarls and growls echoing behind me. Death was chasing me.

Death.

I bolted upright in bed a split second before the sound of a bell tore through the silence.

The flap at the entrance to the tent was torn aside. "Get up. We're under attack," Kira yelled, and then ducked back out.

Ash was on his feet in an instant. Jace rolled off the furs and straight into wolf form. Sage pulled me up, and I made a grab for my sword sheath, strapping it on and then tugging on my boots. Ash kissed me hard on the mouth and then leapt for the exit, shifting into wolf form before he hit the ground.

Someone screamed and then we were out in the night, a night lit up in flames and painted in blood.

Chapter Twenty-Three

"**W**atch out!" Sage scooped me into his arms, hitting the ground with me cradled to his chest.

A dark figure sailed over us, a Feral Claw. It spun and came back at us, but I was up and ready. Sage expelled a jet of flame that engulfed the thing's head, and we were moving on to the next one.

Screams rose up to my left. "Where the fuck did they come from?"

"Nate said there were Feral to the east of the forest," Sage replied.

He had, but this seemed so sudden, and the Claws were obviously not prepared for an attack. There was something off about the whole thing. But my attention needed to be on the surroundings, on the threat. Ash and Jace fought tooth to claw in their Claw forms, silver and gold lashing out at the Feral monsters who all seemed to have the same colored coats of dark shaggy brown. Their red eyes and foaming mouths made them easy to pick out.

Where was Logan? He'd left earlier, and he hadn't been in the tent when we'd woken up. Shit. What if he was hurt? Sage had moved up ahead, blocking a Feral from my sight. Protective, powerful, and beautiful, it was hard to tear my gaze away from his rippling muscles lit up by the flame he was producing. Controlled fire, short bursts of flame directed at a single target. He was obviously conscious about the fact we were surrounded by forests and bark and stuff that would make excellent kindling. Someone screamed, and I turned and headed toward the sound, toward the perimeter and the Claw fighting for her life.

Kira wielded twin blades like they were an extension of herself, slashing at the Feral as if she intended to turn him into confetti. She had this, and I was about to skid to a halt and go in another direction when a snarl to my left had me spinning to counter a Feral leaping at me. I dropped low at the crucial moment and eviscerated it, and then scrambled out of the way to make sure I didn't get trapped beneath its weight. A hand grabbed my upper arm, helping me to my feet.

"Thank yo—" Violet eyes, silver hair, and alabaster skin. "Motherfuck—"

Pain bloomed at my temple and the world was swallowed by darkness.

HEADACHE, damn throbbing headache. Violet eyes. Shit! The Vladul's face swam into focus, and I lashed out. He gripped my wrists before I could make contact with his pretty face.

"I don't want to hurt you." His voice was a smooth caress.

"Bullshit. All your kind want to do is hurt others."

Something dark crossed his features, and his sharp jaw tightened. "It may seem that way to you, and I don't have time to convince you otherwise. I just need the key and then you can go."

The key? He wanted the key. He'd tried to take it that first time we'd tangled outside the office building.

"You tracked me for the key?"

"I need it."

"I was unconscious. You could have taken it."

He blinked down at me as if the thought hadn't even crossed his mind.

I sat up against the rough bark of the tree he'd

propped me up against. "You need to work on your thieving skills."

Yes, taunting a Vladul wasn't the brightest move, but anger was like a hot coal in my chest, and the throbbing headache wasn't helping at all.

He held out his hand. "Give it to me."

"No." I lifted my chin. "If you want it, you're going to have to take it off my dead body."

His expression hardened. "I don't want to hurt you, but I will if I have to."

A fission of fear shot down my back. "Why do you want it?"

"That's none of your concern."

Did he know what it did? How far away from the Claw camp were we? Would anyone hear me if I screamed? Did they even know that I was missing?

I needed more information. "How long have I been out?"

His brow furrowed as if he was thrown by the change in topic. "Not long, maybe ten minutes."

So, we couldn't have gone too far, and Ash or Sage would have noticed I'd gone AWOL; they seemed to have one eye on me at all times. Were they looking for me, or had the Feral Claws taken up all their attention?

Wait, where was I?

Metal cages stood open behind the Vladul.

Cages …

I met his gaze. "What was in the cages?"

His smile was tight. "Feral Claws."

The pieces fell into place. Nate's insistence that he get the cure first. He'd lied and said that it was to help Feral to the east of the forest, when all the time the Feral had been here, trapped in cages. Family? Friends? He'd probably thought he was keeping them safe. But barely ten minutes from camp? Not a wise move.

Focus, Eva. "You let them out to cause a diversion."

The Vladul nodded. "I had to get to you some-how." He pressed his lips together. "Now, please, just give me the key, and you can go back to your friends, help them prevent more deaths."

"What the fuck do you care about how many innocent Claws die?"

His eyes narrowed. "You don't know me. You don't know anything about me."

"And I don't want to know. Like I said. If you want the key, you're going to have to take it."

My hand hovered at my pocket, over the slight bulge of my penknife as he stalked toward me. That's it, fucker, come closer. He came to a standstill and crouched right in front of me.

"Last chance," he said.

"Fuck you."

He made a grab for me, hands going for my

throat, for the leather strap that held the key to me. I wound an arm around his neck, yanking him close enough to inhale his odor, crisp and clean, then slipped the penknife from my pocket, bringing it up to slam into his side in a series of short, sharp jabs.

He grunted in pain, and I shoved him away. He staggered back, clutching the wound, eyes wide with shock, and I ran.

I didn't get far.

He grabbed my hair, yanking me back and smashing me into the tree trunk I'd just been propped up against before pinning me to the bark with a hand at my throat.

His irises were ringed in crimson. "I really wish you hadn't done that."

And then he bit me.

The shock numbed the pain for a second and then my blood was on fire, limbs thrashing as I tried to get away, away from the bite, the sting, the fire. I pressed at his wide shoulders, needing to push him away, but my hands slipped, useless against his granite presence. He was like a wall, unyielding and cold. He was like a parasite, desperate and hungry.

Cold.

So cold.

Images flitted through my mind, purple velvet and golden hair, the creamy column of a throat and a resonant female laugh. The clatter of hooves followed by the baying of an angry mob, and then the slash of a knife and a starlit sky. So bright. So cold.

So cold.

"No!" A voice brimming with rage pulled me back into myself, and the Vladul was gone.

With nothing to hold me up, my body slid to the ground, limp and weak and tingling as if trying desperately to summon a spark. My breath was shallow and fast. Not enough oxygen. Not enough blood to carry the damn oxygen.

Two figures fought to my right. Metal clanged, curses, growls, and hisses were traded. Vanilla ... Logan.

I closed my eyes. Logan, thank God. He'd come to save me, the fragile human. Laughter bubbled up my throat as death hovered at my back.

Too weak.

"Eva! Oh, God." Sage's heat enveloped me as he tugged me away from the chilly earth and cradled me to his chest. "Eva, stay with me."

Something fluttered inside me, an errant, lonely flame. It flickered with every breath, leaning toward Sage.

His hand was on my cheek. "Please, open your eyes."

Dammit, I was trying, but my lids were lead weights.

"We need Ash," Logan said. "Find Ash. I got this."

"What the fuck?" Kira's voice drifted on the wind.

The air whispered across my skin, leaves crunching far away. We were running. Floating.

"Ash! Ash, where's Ash?" Sage sounded frantic, his heart hammering in my ear.

Hush, it's okay. We're okay.

Don't go softly into the night, Eva.

Tobias?

"Logan said you could help her." Sage's gravelly voice shook with emotion.

Cedar wrapped itself around me and warm, dry lips brushed over my parted ones. Sweet breath. Ash's sweet breath and Sage's warm arms. He sealed our mouths, and the heat of euphoria washed through me, tingling through my limbs and dispelling the pins and needles. My shallow breath evened out and my eyelids fluttered open to see his dark lashes brushing my cheek and the frown marring his forehead.

"She's awake," Sage said. "Thank God, she's awake."

Ash broke the healing kiss and pulled back enough to scan my face. I reached up to touch his cheek as strength flooded my limbs, as the flame that had ignited inside me roared to life, stretching upward and outward.

Sage gasped. "Eva ... I feel your flame."

"Bring him through!" Kira's voice was wound tight with rage.

Fists meeting flesh was followed by a grunt.

They had the Vladul. "I can stand. I need to see."

Sage carefully lowered me to the ground, and Ash's arm went around my waist to steady me. My body pressed to his side for a moment, my hand braced on his taut chest, I looked up at him and nodded. His mouth was turned down, his murderous gaze on the creature held captive behind Sage. One moment, just a moment for my knees to realize they weren't made of jelly.

Another punch, another grunt.

"Kill him," Kira said softly.

"No!" I stepped around Sage to see the silver-haired Vladul, bloody and on his knees.

He met my gaze with dark violet eyes. He was flanked by two huge Claws and Kira stood behind him, blade at the ready. Her face was spattered with blood, and her body seemed to vibrate with rage.

I met the female's eyes. "He's mine."

She gritted her teeth, lip curling to emit a low, menacing growl.

"If he doesn't cooperate, you can have him."

She nodded and lowered her blades.

I walked up to the Vladul and crouched in front of him. "You're in the shit now, Vladul. These Claws are ready to rip you to fucking shreds, and I'm half inclined to let them."

He met my gaze steadily, unflinching, unafraid. "I almost killed you."

The fuck? He sounded … sorry. No. He couldn't be sorry; he was a coldblooded killer.

"Listen very carefully. If you want to live, you'll tell me exactly why you want the key, and you'll tell me everything you know about the internal security of the Genesis Foundation."

He cocked his head. "You plan to infiltrate the Foundation."

I arched a brow. "My plans are none of your concern."

He tucked in his chin. "I'm not afraid to die. But I am afraid to leave my people under Malcolm's rule." He raised his head. "I'll tell you what you need to know. I'm not the enemy. I didn't come here to hurt anyone."

"You almost fucking killed her," Sage growled. "Look around. Look what you did."

He kept his eyes on me. "I needed the key."

Yeah, so he kept saying. "Then why the fuck didn't you take it and run when I was knocked out?"

He faltered, his mouth parted as if searching for the words. "I … I don't know."

He was lying. He knew, he just didn't want to say. "Kira, can you set up an interrogation tent please. I just … I need a minute."

"With fucking pleasure," the beta Claw said.

I turned away from the silver-haired Vladul, my eyes searching for the dark-haired Fang that had saved my life. I spotted Jace carrying a sobbing Benji. He raised a hand and then diverted direction to a purple tent, the boy clutched tight to his chest. Oh, God. I hope the boy's aunt was all right.

"Ash says Logan is back at our tent," Sage said.

Once again, Ash knew what I needed, they both did. "Thank you."

I headed toward our tent, weaving past the carnage, the broken, battered remains of a mini war that, thank God, hadn't claimed too many lives, and skirted the dead bodies of the Feral that had been released into our midst.

The tent came into view, still standing by some miracle. I ducked inside to find Logan wiping blood off his bare chest. He looked up sharply as I entered, his mouth parted in surprise, and then he closed his eyes and exhaled through his nose before turning his back on me.

"I thought you were dead." His voice was so soft I barely caught the words.

But I'd seen the flash of relief on his face just before he'd shut it down and turned away. A lump formed in my throat because that look couldn't be found on a face that didn't care. He cared. He fucking cared, and if not for him, I'd be dead. So close, I'd been so close. Another minute, another half a minute and the Vladul would have drained me.

I walked up to his back and then wrapped my arms around him from behind, pressing my cheek to his spine. His shoulder muscles bunched.

I sighed, because why was he fighting this? "You saved my life. Thank you, Logan." I pressed a chaste kiss to his back and then released him and stepped away. "I'm going to be interrogating the Vladul in a few minutes. I'd like it if you could join me."

I slipped from the tent without waiting for a response, without waiting for him to turn to face me, because even though Logan couldn't speak lies, I was done with seeing the lies pasted on his face.

He cared. He fucking cared.

Chapter Twenty-Four

ELIAS

I t couldn't be. It couldn't be, but it was. I'd seen it, felt it, and I'd almost killed her. Once her blood had hit my tongue there had been no stopping. Sweet, so fucking sweet, like nectar, like life. She tasted like life, and I'd almost killed her. The thought turned my blood to ice. Thank God the Fang had stopped me when he had. I could have fought him off easily. He'd been strong, but no match for my Vladul strength, especially with her blood coursing through my veins. But killing him would have alienated her further. He was important to her, they all were. And this was bigger than us all.

Did she know? No, she couldn't, how could she? She was something else, something new, and if I was going to understand it, I'd need to convince her to let me go with them wherever it was they were headed.

I needed time.

The chair I'd been tied to was a flimsy affair. The ropes were nothing, but I sat still and silent, ignoring the blazing Claw eyes on me filled with hatred, and ignoring the reek of pheromones that promised death.

She would come, and somehow I would make her understand.

Chapter Twenty-Five

Kira stood outside the white tent they'd put the Vladul in. She'd wiped the blood off her face but hadn't changed her stained clothes.

"Once you have what you need, then we kill him," she said.

I inclined my head. "Once we have what we need, we kill him." I resisted the urge to touch my neck, the spot he'd sunk his fangs into, the spot that Ash had healed with his kiss. "Can you ask Jace to bring the radio too please?"

Her brows shot up.

"We need to let Noah know what's happening."

She nodded before striding off. I stepped into the tent where two Claws stood glaring at the Vladul. His silver hair looked groomed and sleek despite the tussle, and there wasn't a speck of blood on his face, despite the beating he'd received. No cuts, and no swellings. Damn, he healed fast.

Make the interrogee at ease, throw them off guard. Ah, there you are, Dad.

I crossed my arms under my breasts. "What's your name?"

He looked surprised by the question. "Elias."

Elias. It was a nice name. Too good for one of the likes of them. "I'm Eva."

The air shifted behind me, and the scent of cedar alerted me to Ash's arrival. He walked past me and took a position to the left of Elias, about a meter away. Logan entered a moment later and pulled out a chair from the small table to the right, turned it around, and sat on it, arms resting on the backrest. Jace and Sage entered a second later.

"You have the radio?" I asked Jace.

He frowned. "Was I supposed to bring it?"

Kira obviously hadn't crossed paths with him. "Never mind."

"We're good," Sage said to the Claw sentries, and they ducked out.

Sage and Jace took the sentries' places at the entrance.

Elias took in the getup. Was that a slight smile on his face?

I crossed my arms under my breasts. "You think your predicament is amusing?"

He dropped the smile. "No. Of course not. I apologize for almost draining you. I meant to take enough to heal the wound you inflicted, but your blood is ... intoxicating."

"Yeah, so I've heard."

"I simply wanted the key."

"Why?"

This was where he'd dig in his heels, except this time he didn't.

"To overthrow Malcolm," he said. "He's the Vladul leader and our self-professed king." His lip curled in disgust. "He believes humans should be cattle, to be bred and used as we see fit. He believes Vladul should rule over all other supernatural races."

"And I suppose you don't?" Logan said.

Elias's gaze flicked to the Fang. "No. I don't. That isn't who we are. It isn't who we were meant to be."

Ash made a sound of disgust and shook his head in disbelief.

"We know who you are," Logan said. "We've seen the evidence for the past few decades."

"Yes, under Malcolm's rule," Elias insisted. "Malcolm has the power because he has the key, what we thought was the only key, to the Genesis

Foundation. He can shut it down or make it run. The key accesses the mainframe and can bypass any password or code. If the masses defy him, he can shut us out of the Foundation and leave us to face the Feral in the outside world, or he can program the Feral we have collared to attack us. The Vladul need sanctuary, and just like everyone else, we want to live, so we do as he says and follow his orders handed down by his minions. They call themselves The Enlightened."

"This is bullshit," Logan said.

But there was something in the Vladul's tone, in his eyes, that sparkled with truth and sincerity. "Let him speak, Logan. I want to hear this."

Elias focused on me, his violet eyes wide and clear in the lamplight. "Many centuries ago the Vladul were the protectors of humanity."

Logan let out a bark of laughter.

For fuck's sake. "Logan, please ..." I turned to Sage. "Do you know anything about this? The djinn have been watching our world forever, right?"

Sage's chest rumbled. "I can't say. I've been a watcher for just over a century. The Vladul didn't exist to your world then."

"Like I said," Logan drawled. "Bullshit."

I shot Logan a flat look, then jerked my chin at Elias, indicating he continue.

Elias's jaw flexed; he took a shallow breath

245

through his nose and exhaled through his mouth as if grounding himself. "I know it must seem preposterous to you, but it's true. There was a royal bloodline, there was peace. We coexisted with humans and kept them safe from other supernatural predators. In exchange, humans donated their blood to us. We were the landlords of small villages all over the world. We were the aristocracy of that age, and humans accepted us because they needed us. But then times began to change, technology emerged, and humans created new weapons. They began communicating along vast distances, and their need for our services decreased. The queen wanted to withdraw from civilization, to find a new home where we might live off the blood of animals. But her advisor, her right-hand man, didn't agree."

"Your leader, Malcolm, I presume," Logan said.

"Yes. He'd been building a resistance beneath the queen's nose. A band of Vladul who believed they were the superior race and that humans were cattle. In this time of uncertainty, he was able to rise and overthrow the queen. He not only murdered her but also every Vladul who carried the royal blood, professing that he had freed the Vladul of the shackles of servitude to the creatures beneath them." He paused for a long beat. "The Vladul you know of are the ones that came after. The ones ruled by Malcolm. The ones that raped and pillaged and killed and were finally forced underground when humanity, with its vast numbers and shiny new weapons, turned against them. The few that remained evolved and procreated and became the Fangs that your new society finally welcomed into the fold. But Malcolm is back now. With the world weakened, with humanity decimated and the other supernatural races on the brink of extinction, he has the upper hand, and I have to stop him. I need that key."

His story, as fantastical as it sounded, made sense. He could have killed me while I'd been unconscious and taken the key and run, but he hadn't. He'd said over and over that he meant me no harm.

I blew out a breath. "Why you? Why do you think the Vladul will follow you if you have the key?"

He locked gazes with me. "Because I'm the last of the royal bloods."

"I thought you said Malcolm killed them all."

"He did. All except me. I was just a child, and if he wanted the Vladul to follow him, he needed to show a softer side, a side that said, of course he wasn't a monster, and so he picked me, the queen's sole heir, to live."

He was Vladul royalty?

"The rest of the royal bloodline, first cousins and

second cousins and everyone in between, were purged. He raised me as his own. He kept me safe, and he used me as a symbol of the new order. But no more. My people deserve to be free. We're not monsters, and I won't let Malcolm continue to force us to commit atrocious acts."

"The key will give you power over the stronghold," Sage reiterated.

"Yes," Elias said.

"You can lock Malcolm out. But what about his legion?" Sage said. "They could hunt you down and take the key off you. You're just one Vladul."

The djinn was asking the very questions that were going through my mind.

Elias wasn't fazed, though. He smirked. "Am I?"

He had another ace up his sleeve. "What do you mean?"

"I mean I learned from a master of deception, a man who stood by my mother's side for centuries and lied to her face while building a resistance. I learned that you have to bide your time and prepare."

The penny dropped. "You have a resistance?"

He nodded. "We are vast, and we are everywhere in the Foundation, but until I saw the key around your neck the final piece of the puzzle had been missing. Our coup would have been a huge risk with technology at the ready to smash us down." His gaze fell to my throat. "The key can change everything. Once I have control of the Foundation, the human and supernatural prisoners can be free. We can start over, really start over, and build a new world."

"Are you buying this?" Logan asked me.

Ash signed rapidly, and Logan made a sound of exasperation.

"Eva?" Logan asked me again.

"What did Ash say?"

"I want to know what you think first."

Ash was looking at me too. I could feel his attention warm on my face, but I kept my eyes on Elias.

"I think you're telling me the truth. I think your plan and intentions are solid. But I can't give you the key."

He sagged in his seat and tucked in his chin. "I was really hoping we could resolve this amicably, that you'd understand. But it looks like I'm just going to have to take it."

He exploded out of the chair and headed straight for me. Logan and Ash both leapt to intercept him, but he threw them both off, intent on getting to me. Jace pulled me out of the way, and Sage took my place, colliding with the Vladul. They tussled, and damn if they weren't head to head. Logan was back on his feet and so was Ash; they grabbed Elias, pinning his arms behind his back, but he slipped out of their grasp, moving so fast he was impossible to track. Jace yelped and then Elias had me in a throat hold, my back against his chest, breath hot in my ear.

"Move one step and I'll crack her neck," Elias said.

Ash growled deep in his throat, and Logan's lip curled in a snarl, but Sage was studying the Vladul carefully. He was reading his colors. I arched a brow, and he shook his head infinitesimally.

Elias's grip was firm, tight but not painful. "You won't hurt me. That isn't who you are. If it was, you'd have killed me already."

"Damn you." He released me and shoved me away.

I slowly turned to face him, and it was just the two of us, staring each other down. He could have escaped at any time, he could have knocked Logan out by the cages and taken the key then. So why? Why hadn't he? There was more to his story, more to him. He waited, allowing me to process these facts. He was royalty, he was a new hope, and he had information in his head about the inside of the Foundation. He was essential, and if he wanted, he had the speed to rip the key from my neck and run, and yet he remained stationary, his gaze fixed on my face, my lips, my eyes, my hair. Heat crawled up my neck.

I swallowed. "If you really believe in changing things, in bringing down this Malcolm, then you'll leave the key with me, at least for now."

He frowned. "Why would I do that?"

"Because the key unlocks the cure to the virus. A cure that could change everything."

His mouth parted in shock. "A cure ... That's where you're headed? To get this cure?"

"Yes."

"Dammit, Eva," Logan said. "Why not share our secret bunker location too. I'm sure the Vladul would love to drop in for a fucking visit."

I ignored him, focusing on Elias, focusing on controlling my erratic pulse because this was big. The cure, him, the whole backstory and the possibilities. If we could work together.

Elias was considering. "I'm coming with you."

Yes!

"Like hell you are." Kira stood in the doorway.

I turned to face her, but a figure rose up behind her — Nate in his furs, all steely-eyed and intense.

"The Vladul belongs to us," Nate said. "He owes us a blood debt, and the souls of our dead will be avenged."

Oh, shit. I held up my hands. "Look, this is bigger than us. Elias knows the Foundation inside out. He's a walking schematic to that place, and once we have the cure, he'll be invaluable to our infiltration."

Okay, so Elias hadn't agreed to any of this, but fuck it, he'd just have to go along with me.

"First-name basis now?" Kira's tone was laced with disgust. "What happened to the interrogation?"

"There's no need for force when the interrogee cooperates," Jace said softly.

Kira's lips tightened. "Get the information you need. That was the deal."

"The information we need is in his head," Sage said. "It's not something we can simply extract and take with us."

"Then he's useless."

She was being pigheaded. "Seriously? Are you not listening to anything we're saying?"

It was Nate who responded. "Two Claws are dead, and the Feral ..." His tone dropped as if in reverence. "We were forced to slaughter them all."

So that was what this was about? "Well, then maybe you shouldn't have fucking kept them caged up less than ten minutes from the camp."

He flinched and turned his hot glare on me. "Are you intimating that this is my fault?"

"I'm *intimating* that you're partially to blame. It was a dumb move, despite your reasons, and what Elias did was seize an opportunity to get what he needed to save his people. Everyone is fucking doing what they need to do to protect their own, and it's about time we stopped and focused on the bigger picture." I stepped away from Elias. "You want to kill him, then fine. I won't stand in your way. Kill him, but it won't bring back the dead. What it *will* do is end our best chance of infiltrating the Foundation."

Nate's eyes were narrowed, his jaw working.

"Nate?" Kira asked.

Nate closed his eyes and exhaled slowly. "Take him. Take him and get out of my camp. Now."

"Nate?" Kira looked shocked.

"Get them to where they need to be, Kira." Nate swept from the tent.

Kira bowed her head. "You have no idea how much that just cost him. His son and his wife were two of the Feral we were just forced to kill."

My heart sank. "I'm sorry. I truly am, and trust me, I don't excuse what Elias did, but I can't deny that given the same circumstances, I would have done the same."

She fixed her gaze on Elias. "You better be worth it, Vladul. One false move and I *will* end you."

He didn't reply.

"Get your shit together and meet me at the gates in ten minutes," she snapped.

Relief flooded through me at her exit, and I

turned to face Elias. "Let us down and she won't be the one sticking a knife in your throat."

Was that amusement in his gaze? "I won't betray you, Eva."

Damn, my name on his lips sounded way too intimate. I dismissed him in favor of Ash. "I'll grab our stuff from the tent and meet you at the gates." I looked to Jace. "We should call Noah and give him an update too."

"I tried," Jace said. "He's not picking up."

In that case, we'd just have to hope we'd made the right decision. The cure was mere hours away, and we were traveling with the enemy.

LOGAN FOUND me in the tent a few minutes later.

I sighed. "I know; you think I'm making a mistake."

He gathered the weapons. "I don't know, Eva. My powers don't work on Vladul or other Fangs, otherwise I'd look into his head and make him spill all his secrets."

"I think he's telling us the truth, but I'm in no doubt that there's stuff he's hiding."

"I'm sorry," Logan said.

I faced him. "What for? For saving my life?"

He offered me a lopsided smile. "No. Not sorry

about that." His expression sobered. "I'm sorry for storming out earlier, for not getting to you sooner, and … I'm sorry for being so sharp with you."

Wow. "I'll take it." I strapped my sword on. "I get that you just want to protect Ash. I get that I'm an unwanted variable in your world. But I'm not going anywhere, not if I can help it, so it would be nice if we could just … get along."

Damn, why was my heart beating so fast. Could he hear it? Of course he could.

His brow furrowed slightly, and he reached up to brush his thumb lightly along my cheek. "Get along … But Eva, don't you get it? That's what I'm afraid of."

He cared.

Shit. He really cared.

The pulse in my throat was fluttering like mad, and breathing was suddenly too hard.

His throat bobbed, and he dropped his hand from my cheek and took a step back.

My breath whooshed out of my lungs. "We should get going. We have a cure to get."

Chapter Twenty-Six

After the long journey on foot, after the fighting and the pain, the van drive was alien and disconcerting. I sat cushioned between Ash and Sage. Jace and Logan sat opposite me, and Elias was tucked at the back overseen by Kira. The Claw refused to take her eyes off him.

There was no need for the vigilance. Sage would warn me if Elias's colors shifted, if he intended to do harm, run, or be deceitful. It was strange, because when he'd been speaking it had been as if I could hear the honesty wrapped around each syllable.

He wasn't the threat. Malcolm was. And we were almost at the first stop to victory. Apprehension skittered across my skin like a colony of ants, and *what ifs* rose up in my mind. What if we were wrong? What if we were too late? What if the cure wasn't a cure at all but a vaccine to prevent infection like Jace had proposed?

But *what ifs* would drive me crazy.

Sage sandwiched my hand between his, and then ran his thumb over the back of mine soothingly. I sighed and forced my mind to let go and relax. My eyes drifted closed, and my head fell onto Ash's hard shoulder; he shifted position to wrap an arm around me and pull me against his chest, and I had the rhythm of his heartbeat to lull me into sleep.

The van rocked and bumped and dipped and my body drifted into a much-needed doze. But the world around me was still on alert, and the voices and sounds still trickled into my ears.

"How much longer till we get to the coordinates?" Logan asked.

"Please don't tell me you're going to be asking me if we're there yet every few minutes," Kira said.

"No." Logan's tone was brusque. "I asked how long we had left on the journey."

Footsteps followed by the slide of metal on metal. "Carter, what's our ETA?"

"An hour out, Kira."

"There, you happy?"

"Peachy."

Silence reigned, or had I slipped into a deeper sleep?

"Eva?" Sage's rumble of a voice. "We're approaching our stop off now."

Sleep slipped away and energy flooded my body. We were here? I'd slept the whole way. The van ground to a halt, and Kira opened the side door. We piled out into the early morning light and stared at the building crowded by huge trees.

The air was thinner here.

"We're up a mountain," Sage explained. "The van almost didn't make the steep drive. They didn't make it easy to get to this place."

The building was squat and low to the ground. No windows but there were cameras high up, pointed down at us. They tracked our approach.

"You think they're on auto?" Logan asked.

"Unlikely," Jace said. "That would require power to have been left on for the past few decades. I don't see a source of water here so not sure the power would be hydraulic."

"A generator?" Kira suggested.

"It would have to be one heck of an epic generator, and there'd have to be someone here to man it."

Someone here? "Maybe there is."

"The generator at the Foundation is self-sustaining," Elias said. "No maintenance required, as the fossil fuel that runs it is unlike anything we've ever seen. The scientists that were at the Foundation when we took it said that it was a new source of energy, one that the government had been keeping under wraps."

Figured. There had been way too much the government had neglected to share with the general public.

We began walking toward the doors. A scuffle behind me was followed by a thud and scrape. I turned to see Elias picking himself off the ground with Bates, one of Kira's men, standing over him with a shit-eating grin on his face.

Elias's jaw was clenched in suppressed anger.

I pushed past Carter to get to his comrade. "You serious?" I was toe to toe with the Claw. "You think that's funny?"

Bates's expression morphed to disgust. "What? You want to take him into your little harem?"

Heat crawled up my chest. "What if I do? Huh? You got a problem with that?"

"He just tried to kill you."

"NO. No, he didn't. If he had, I'd be dead. In fact, if he'd wanted to, he could have knocked you on your arse a second ago. If he wanted to, he could have fought off your guards at the camp and made a getaway. He's a fucking Vladul. The first race. One of the first fucking vampires, and he's royalty, you twat."

Bates flinched as if I'd spat in his face. Heck, maybe I had. "Touch him again and I won't be responsible for his actions." I turned away from him and pushed back to the front of the group. "He's with us. He's one of us. We're no longer Claw, or Fang, Vladul or djinn, we're a fucking team. Bigger picture, guys. Get with the program or piss off."

Bates muttered something.

"Shut the fuck up," Kira snapped. "Stay with the van. You too, Carter."

We reached the metal doors, closed tight against the outside world. No hand, no panel, no place for a key to go.

"Um, how the fuck do we get in?" Logan asked the question on all our minds.

I looked up at the camera fixed above the door, at the single red winking light. If someone was in there, watching, maybe they'd been waiting for Dad, for the key.

A tug on the leather strap around my neck had the key visible. I held it up to the camera.

"My name is Eva Williams. My father was Dr. Frederick Williams. He gave me this before he died, and I believe he wanted me to bring it here."

No one interrupted, and after I'd finished speaking, there was silence. The air was tense with anticipation. Long seconds ticked by and nothing happened.

"Dammit," Kira said. "What no—"

A *clang* and a *whirr*. The ground rumbled beneath our feet and the door began to slide open. My pulse sped up as an inky darkness bloomed beyond the doors.

"Not empty after all," Elias said.

The door was halfway open when I stepped through. There was someone here, someone who'd been waiting for me.

"Carter, keep tabs on the radio," Kira said.

The others entered at my back. Logan and Ash stepped up to flank me as we stood in the dark entranceway and then with a *buzz* and *putter* the lights came on. We were in a small, square room painted magnolia with the open door at our backs and a closed one in front of us. The door in front was metal but fit seamlessly into the wall. Airtight.

"What is this?" Kira asked.

I glanced up, noting the long vents in the ceiling. It was obvious what this room was for.

"Decontamination chamber," Elias said, beating me to it.

He pointed to the vents, and his long-sleeved shirt tugged tight over his chest. What was that fabric? It seemed to mold to him like a second skin. Some kind of smart material maybe?

The door behind us slid closed smoothly—eerie because it had taken ages to open.

"I don't like this." Kira's tone dipped low to communicate her disquiet.

There was an ominous hiss and then the room was filled with a misty gas that coated my skin and invaded my airways.

"It's fine," Elias said. "Don't panic. They have this stuff at the Foundation too."

It lasted several seconds and then dissipated in favor of another drier gas which pelted us harshly. My hair whipped back, and my eyes closed instinctively against the assault.

Then it was over, leaving me breathless and tingling.

"Fuck." Jace swept a hand through his hair, pushing it off his forehead and out of his eyes.

"I think that's it," Elias said. "Whoever is inside should let us in now."

The door in front of us opened into another chamber, the same size as the previous one. There was a panel on the wall and a speaker high up in the crease of the ceiling and wall. No vents here, thank goodness.

The door behind us closed with a *whoosh*.

"Welcome to Genesis," a mechanical voice said. "Seven life forms detected. Please step up to the panel and place your thumb to the glass."

"Okay. Now what is this?" Kira asked.

"I'm not sure," Jace said. "It can't be for identification purposes, because if it is, we're fucked."

"There's only one way to find out." I stepped up to the panel and pressed my thumb to it. There was a sharp sting that had me pulling away from the glass. "Shit, it stabbed me."

The mechanical voice greeted me again. "Blood analysis in progress."

"Checking for the virus?" Logan suggested.

"Yeah, that makes sense." I sucked on my thumb to soothe the sting.

"I'll go next," Logan said, stepping up so he was abreast of me.

His arm brushed mine as he reached for the panel, but before he could make contact the door swished open.

"Okay, that was strange," Elias said. "Doesn't it want to test the rest of us?"

He had a point. But we'd come this far and there was no going back, because without this opportunity, there was nowhere to go.

I crossed the threshold into the corridor beyond, white and clean and gleaming. Clinical and fresh like the hospital wing at the compound. It even had the antiseptic smell to it.

"Welcome to Genesis, please follow the lights," the mechanical voice said.

Lights?

The bulb above us switched to green, and then

the next and the next. Okay, *that* light. We followed the green light as it skipped from bulb to bulb, down the corridor without any windows or doors, and to a lift, wide open and welcoming.

"Please enter the lift."

Was there a hint of excitement to the mechanical tone now? No. How could anything mechanical get excited? Unless … Unless it wasn't mechanical? The frown on Ash's face as we crammed into the lift echoed my disquiet. The Fang remained close to me, his breath stirring the hair at my crown.

"I said it twice and I'll say it again," Kira said. "I don't like this."

The lift doors closed, and my stomach did a flip as we began to descend. Shit, how far down were we headed? I reached for Ash's hand, and he wrapped his fingers around mine and tugged me closer. Kira's disquiet was contagious, because now my gut was sending all kinds of *beware* signals to my brain. But Dad wouldn't have sent me here if it was dangerous. I blew out a breath, gave Ash's hand a squeeze, and then let go to signal I was okay.

The lift came to a shuddering halt, and the doors opened directly into what looked like a high-tech lab. Sleek chrome and glass and equipment that I had no names for filled the space.

"Bloody hell." Jace was the first to exit, walking into the room to examine a machine to our left.

Kira stepped out behind him. Logan went next, then Sage and Ash. Elias waited, sweeping a hand out to indicate I go first. There was that smile on his lips again, secretive and knowing, as if he was hiding something I was meant to know. I brushed by him into the lab and felt him right behind me. The hairs on the nape of my neck quivered at the proximity, and I hastily walked farther into the room to stand by Sage.

"Hello?" I tilted my chin, looking for more cameras. "Anyone here?"

"Well, well, well, haven't you grown." A figure stepped out as if from nowhere.

Brown hair, spectacles, and a lopsided smile greeted me. My heart slammed against my ribcage so hard it would be impossible for the others not to hear it.

I took a stumbling step toward the figure. "Dad? How ... How is this possible?"

He made an 'o' with his mouth and then winced. "I'm afraid there's been some confusion, Eva. I'm not your father, at least not the one that raised you, although I am him in every other way."

"I don't understand. What are you saying?"

"He's a clone," Jace said softly.

The man that looked like my father glanced across at Jace and pointed a finger. "Bingo. Well done. Somebody give the boy a lollipop. Bravo, Jeeves."

What the fuck?

He rubbed his hands together. "I've been waiting forever, and now you're here in all your glory, bringing your wonderful blood. Fantastic."

My blood? "What are you talking about? What about my blood."

He pressed his lips together and squeezed his eyes shut. "Wait, wait. I need to rein it in. Frederick was very clear—give the background first."

"My dad spoke to you?" I hated the tremor in my voice.

"Your dad was the one that made me. He cloned himself so that he could work faster, more efficiently on the cure. This was our haven. Our lab for most of the time. He would flit between here and the Foundation, leaving me to continue our work in secret." He placed a hand to his mouth and giggled. "They never knew what we were up to. He didn't want them to know. He didn't trust their motives or their methods." He walked around a counter, fingers trailing over the sterile surface. "It was right here that we finally came across the right combination."

"You synthesized a cure here?" Jace asked.

He blinked rapidly, his gaze tracking to me, setting in motion a flutter of crazy butterflies in my stomach because my puzzler's brain was putting together the pieces and not liking the picture.

"We didn't synthesize the cure," Dad's clone said. "But we created the organism that would eventually do so." He smiled at me. "We created you, Eva."

Chapter Twenty-Seven

We *created you, Eva.*
    Created Eva.
    Created …

The world tilted on its axis and sturdy hands grabbed me, steadying me and pulling me to the heat of a familiar chest. Ash. Oh, thank God.

Created.

"Eva?" Logan's face swam before my eyes. "Come on. Snap out of it."

He sounded annoyed, but that was his customary setting, and right now it was exactly what I needed to knock the shock out of my system and plant me back into the driver's seat. This had to be a mistake.

Get it together, Eva.

I tugged the key from around my neck, snapping

the leather to free it from my body, and held it out. "This is the key to the cure. This key unlocks it. Dad told me to bring it here."

The clone's smile was reflective. "The drive to unravel, the need for knowledge, and a noble heart which will need to be circumvented—we knew about all these traits when we put you together."

"Stop saying that."

"I'm sorry. I suppose it must be a strange notion to accept. The key was always meant as a talisman to get you to me, an initial identifier if, and only if, Frederick perished. His goal was to make sure you lived and teach you to survive. He was to teach you to trust no one and to fight tooth and nail to get here. You made it, but not alone. You came surrounded by allies." He shook his head. "Nature prevailed, it seemed."

None of this was making sense, or maybe it was, but I didn't want it to.

"You were our last hope," the clone said. "A prayer. And up until now, just a few moments ago, I wasn't even sure our prayers had been answered. But the proof is here, in your blood. I infected the sample we took at the doors and the antibodies appeared immediately to eradicate the virus. We have it. We have the essential ingredient to create a cure."

The cure. The thing we'd come this far for, the

thing that had been with me all along. My blood. Mine.

I swallowed the lump in my throat and fought back the rising panic. "What am I?"

His brow crinkled. "Wait, did I not say?"

He tapped his chin with an index finger as if running the previous few minutes of conversation through his mind. How long had he been here alone? At least as long as I'd been alive, that was for sure. Almost nineteen years.

He made an apologetic face. "No, no, I didn't say. So sorry. You're a chimera, Eva. The combinations of several zygotes from different supernatural species. Your foundation was human and the rest …"

I held up a hand. "Stop. *What* am I exactly?"

"Oh, um, let me see. Djinn, a dash of Vladul, some Fang, and quite a bit of fey. We combined it all and wrapped it in a human package. Frederick created a DNA marker to stabilize it all, and voila, we had you." He smiled. "Frederick was a genius. I honestly didn't think we'd be able to create a marker to stabilize the DNA, but he did it. He found a solution, and he made it work. We created you, the perfect machine to synthesize a cure."

"She's not a fucking machine," Jace said.

I looked across at him in surprise to see him practically vibrating with anger. He never lost his temper, not so far as I'd seen, but right now he looked as if he wanted to slam a fist into the clone's face.

The clone held up both hands. "I apologize, of course. It's been a long few years alone, and, um, I suppose social etiquette isn't really my forte."

Jace simmered down slightly, his shoulders unknotting, but his fists remained clenched. "Go on."

"Right, okay. You have to understand that all other experimentation at the Foundation had failed."

"Yes, we know," Logan said. "You're looking at three of the failures."

"Oh, really? Oh, how fascinating. Yes, yes. I would love to, um …"

Logan glared at him.

The clone winced. "Right … probably not the … Anyway, every hybrid we'd created and then infected with the virus perished. Eva was our last hope." He focused on me with my dad's warm brown eyes, except they weren't my dad's eyes, they belonged to a version of him that had never known me. "We extracted a sample of your blood because we didn't want to infect you directly; no, we weren't going to replicate the Foundation's horrific practices. You were a person now, and we were determined to treat you as such."

He sounded like he was reciting a quote. One he'd reiterated to himself on many occasions. Were they his words or my father's?

"We infected the blood with the virus," he continued. "The virus and your blood cells interacted, and we saw the beginnings of a possible antibody, but in the end, the virus won. Frederick ran some tests and hypothesized that time was what you needed. Time for your body to mature, for your immune system to grow stronger. Time for the genes we'd built you with to begin to have an effect on your overall makeup."

"What do you mean? Take effect?" Sage asked.

The clone's eyes darkened in the way that happens before someone is about to deliver bad news, and my stomach clenched in anticipation. What more? What more could he throw at me.

"The marker we placed inside Eva to stabilize her DNA was always a temporary measure. The combination of genes we used wasn't meant to exist, and nature, as always, will take its course and destroy any true abominations." He broke eye contact with Sage to settle on me again and my mouth was suddenly dry. "We'd synthesized you from scratch. You weren't born from a template, you weren't birthed from two templates, you were a patchwork of supernatural power."

"Spit it out," Logan said.

"We calculated the lifespan of the stabilizer as nineteen to twenty years. In between this time, Frederick was sure your blood would be ready to fight off the virus, as the stabilizer would have begun to break down, allowing the other genes to influence your blood. I've studied your bloodwork, and the marker is indeed dissolving; you have maybe a month left before it breaks down and the supernatural genes inside you begin their war for dominion over your body."

"And then what?" I forced the words out, knowing what was coming and hating myself for needing to hear it spelled out.

"And then ... It will kill you."

His words were like stones settling over my heart, and a strange numbness spread through me.

"She's dying?" Logan's voice rose an octave in disbelief. "No. No. Fuck you. You can do something. You can fix this."

"I'm sorry." The clone backed up. "There's nothing I can do."

"Ash, no." Jace stepped into Ash's path and pressed a palm to his chest. "Dammit, hurting him won't help Eva."

Dying. I was dying.

But you can save everyone else before you go. Don't fall at the last hurdle, sweetheart. You can do this.

Fuck you, Dad. Fuck you.

Anger flared in my chest, fury toward the man who'd raised me, who'd lied to me, who'd created me, and for what? To be used and discarded. To be a machine to synthesize a cure. To be nothing but what was in my blood? In that moment, there was nothing but hatred toward that man.

But he's gone, Tobias whispered. *And you are what you are. Think of all the lives, Eva.*

His voice in my head was the best of me, the noble heart, the warrior, and the lover. His voice was the hidden parts of me that had been denied all these years by another voice, the voice of a liar, the voice of a man who'd claimed to love me with all his heart knowing I was nothing more than a collection of cells sewn together for a fate that I would never see the benefits of.

Ash tried to sidestep Jace, and Sage joined him, advancing toward the clone of my dad as if hurting him would change anything.

"Don't." I didn't raise my voice, but the guys halted immediately. "Jace is right, hurting him won't save me." I fixed my attention on my dad's clone. "How long will it take to make enough of the vaccine using my blood?"

He smiled softly. "I can see Frederick did a great job of raising a noble, brave woman."

Brave? Fuck, he had no idea. My insides were quivering, and the urge to scream was trapped at the base of my throat, but yeah, we'd go with brave for now.

I blinked back the heat gathering behind my eyes. I'd be damned if I'd break down now. "We should get to work, but before you do you need to know that the virus may have mutated. Humans are turning Feral. We'll need to go out and find one, get you a blood sample so you can extract the mutated virus."

"No need." He puffed out his chest. "I have what we need. I've been taking short excursions outside, sunlight and fresh air, you know." He ducked his head. "Frederick said not to, but ..."

He'd disregarded the warning and taken a sojourn that could have gotten him killed. It could have meant there was no one to synthesize the fucking cure, and all for a little sunshine. But from the look on his face, he knew all this.

My smile was strained. "It's okay, because you're okay. I assume you came across a Feral human?"

"Yes. I was attacked two days ago. The Feral had made it halfway up the mountain. I put him out of his misery and took some samples. I'll need to make two batches of the cure, one to combat the original virus and hopefully one that can take care of the mutated version."

I exhaled in relief. "Good. Real good."

He winced. "There is one other teensy thing."

"What now?"

He wrung his hands. "So, just to clarify, the vaccine is also a cure. The reason the Feral are, well, feral, is because the virus is inside them mutating their genes and blocking access to parts of their brain that would give them higher reasoning. The cure will eradicate the virus and act as a vaccine for those that are uninfected, creating immunity. But the quickest, surest way to dispense it is as an airborne agent. It was what the Foundation had planned, and they have the drones to do it. Hundreds of drones preprogramed with routes. They have the facility to replicate the cure a hundredfold and—"

"Wait," Sage interrupted. "Are you saying you can't make enough of the cure here?"

"That's exactly what he's saying," Jace said in disgust.

"This facility is a small research base. I just don't have the equipment. But the Foundation—"

"Is overrun with Vladul," Logan said. "We can't just waltz in there and ask to borrow their equipment."

The guys were in rage mode—their stances, their tone, the very air crackled with it, and it really wasn't to do with the possibility of having to go back to the Foundation. No, this was to do with my imminent demise.

Laughter, totally inappropriate and uncalled for, clawed at my throat. Dammit. Not now. Instead, I focused on the plan— on my blood, which was the cure; on Elias, who was our way into the Foundation; and on Sage, who was our armory.

Time for a reality check. "We were going to infiltrate the Foundation anyway. We'll just have to do it sooner."

"Without the manpower curing the Feral would have given us." Sage shook his head.

"We have the Claws," Kira said. "And there are two Fang bases we can contact for help."

Sage rubbed his jaw. "Maybe."

"And you have me," Elias said. "I can map the place out for you. I can get in and disable the security systems."

We could do this. They knew we had a real shot. *Dying.*

No time to think about that. "Let's get to work. I need you to make as much of the cure as you can. We need to make sure we have backups in case."

The clone nodded. "I'll take some more blood, and then you can rest. It will take an hour or so to make the cure."

I rolled up my sleeve. "Take what you need."

FREDERICK, my father, had named his clone Jamie, and now Jamie had my blood.

He pocketed the vials and smiled. "The door to the left will take you to the cabins; we have five, so you may have to share, but you should get some rest." He patted my shoulder, and I resisted the urge to pull away. "The more you exert yourself, the faster the deterioration will occur."

His matter-of-fact tone made my heart ache.

"Thanks for the warning." There was no hiding the bitterness to my tone.

I closed my eyes and reined it in, willing numbness to take its place, because why rage about something that I had no control over?

Jamie retreated through a door at the back of the lab, leaving me with my back to the guys.

"I should go out and bring in Carter and Bates," Kira said. "Let them get some rest, and then we can make a plan as to where to go from here."

Her boot falls retreated.

"Eva, we need to talk about this," Jace said softly.

I turned to face them with a tight smile. "Let's get some rest, then we can plan strategy."

Jace and Logan exchanged glances.

"Fuck strategy," Logan said. "We need to discuss how we can save you."

"You can't. Jamie made that clear. This is it.

This was my purpose, and I've served it. I'd like to see it come to fruition, though." Saying the words out loud were like stabbing myself in the chest with a knitting needle. No. I needed numbness. I needed the calm. "I'm going to take a nap." I headed for the door.

"You're going to give up?" Logan called after me.

"Logan ..." Sage's tone held a warning.

"No," Logan replied. "She doesn't get to give up. This isn't how this—"

I slammed the door on his words and headed down the bland corridor and into the first cabin to my right. Stay serene, stay calm. Sleep and function and get this shit done. Get the cure out there, and then ... whatever happens, happens.

Fear reared its ugly head.

No.

Go the fuck away.

Not now, not ever.

The door behind me opened and closed. "Seriously? You're going to do *this*?"

"Go away, Logan." My monotone echoed my emotions.

Hard hands gripped my shoulders and spun me round. "Look at me. Look at me, dammit."

I raised my eyes to his glittering, angry ones. "What?"

DEBBIE CASSIDY

"You don't get to do this. You don't get to come into our lives, turn it inside out, and then just check out."

My voice was even and unemotional. "It's not like I have a choice. I'm dying. Best to accept it and focus on the things we can make a difference on."

"You *do* have a choice. You have the choice to fight to live."

A spark of irritation broke through the self-imposed numbness. "Why the fuck do you even care? You've made it clear time and time again that you want me gone. Well guess what, now you get your wish."

His face went through a series of emotions, so quick they were hard to catch and decipher, and then he was yanking my head back by the hair, eliciting an involuntary yelp.

"You want to know what I wish? What I really fucking wish?"

The answer was in his grip, in the murky, swirling depths of his dark eyes.

No. I didn't. I didn't want to hear it. "Don't."

The corner of his mouth lifted. "Oh, Eva, we are so past that." His mouth crushed mine in a punishing kiss.

The heat that had been gathering behind my eyes melted to tears. "No!" I tore my mouth from him. "No. You don't get to do this. Not now. I can't. I won't."

He kissed me again, hard and desperate and hungry, as if trying to cram a hundred kisses into one. My heart swelled in my chest, and the numbness threatened to retreat. I shoved at his immovable torso, wanting him gone, but in the next heartbeat, I fisted his shirt, pulling him closer.

He moaned into my mouth, tongue deep, and pushed me up against the desk. One hand still tangled in my hair, he used the other to skim, rough and needy, over my body. He kneaded my breast then moved round to cup and squeeze my ass. He was claiming me, leaving a trail of delicious flames in the wake of his rough touch. There was fire in my veins, forcing me awake, but waking hurt. Waking meant facing the truth. It meant really facing my fate.

I shoved him away, struggling to find the breath to speak. "Why are you doing this? Why now? Damn you, Logan. I'm dying. Do you get that? It's over."

His mouth turned down in anger and his free hand pinched my chin, forcing me to look at him. "It's only over if you give up. And I won't let you. I won't let you tear into my life and force my heart to beat again only to crush it. You don't get to fucking check out. You *have* to live."

How dare he, how dare he show his hand now when it was too late. "Maybe I don't want to fight."

"No?" He arched a brow and then he kissed me hard and rough—a passionate crush of lips—before spinning me away from him and pulling my back to his chest. "You don't want to live?" His hand slid down my abdomen toward my waistband.

Oh, God. My body was alive and aching for this. "Fuck you, Logan."

"No, Eva. Fuck you." With one deft move he yanked down my slacks and pushed me down over the desk.

One huge hand pinned me to the wood and the other pulled down my panties and cupped me. I was wet for him, ready for the slide of his fingers as they slipped over my throbbing need.

Oh, God. Oh, fucking God.

"You want to die?" He adjusted the rhythm, making me squirm and gasp. "You want to not feel?"

Oh, shit. Oh, fuck. My body was taking over, moving against his fingers, helping him to set the pace, a pace that would shatter me.

"Logan, please …"

"Fuck you, Eva." His voice was raw, and then his hand was gone and his dick pressed against my entrance.

I pushed back, and he sucked in a breath through his teeth. "Goddamn you."

He entered me with a single thrust. There was a burn—part pain, part pleasure—as he stretched me. He rocked his hips against my ass, rubbing against the spot, the fucking delicious spot that was spiraling me, tightening me, forcing me to claw at the desk and rock hard against him.

"Dammit, Eva. Shit." He gripped the back of my neck, his fingers unyielding. "Don't. Fucking. Move."

My body went completely still at his command.

"Good girl. That's right." His voice was a raw purr.

The pressure was there, nirvana was there, just out of reach. I needed this, I needed him to … "Logan, please …"

"Please what? Say it, Eva?"

I squeezed my eyes shut, hating myself. Hating him. Wanting him. "Please, fuck me."

"With pleasure." He started to roll his hips against mine, building the pressure, winding me tighter. And then he began to thrust, long, powerful thrusts, harder and faster. Blood roared in my ears as sensation built and gathered, ready to explode. It shot outward, down my legs and my arms, until there was only the crashing wave and the ride as I bucked with the orgasm, my cry of release a shameful, wonderful thing.

Long moments passed and then his chest pressed to my back and his mouth brushed my earlobe. "That's what you're giving up, Eva. Life, sensation, my cock inside you. You're a fighter, a survivor, so fucking fight."

He withdrew, and a moment later the door opened and shut.

He was gone, and I was left trembling with the memory of his touch.

Chapter Twenty-Eight

ELIAS

Eva slammed the door behind her, leaving nothing but stunned silence in her wake.

"We have to do something," the Fang named Jace said. "There has to be a way to save her."

"Just because Jamie doesn't know how doesn't mean there isn't someone who does," the huge djinn said. Sage, that was his name.

They were right, of course they were right. "The Foundation has some of the most high-tech equipment in the world at its disposal and some of the brightest minds. Once we have it under our control, we can set them to work on the problem."

"That's provided she lasts that long," the dark-eyed Fang said softly. "You saw her face, she's given up. She's accepted she's going to die. Half the battle against any sickness is psychological."

"This isn't a sickness," the djinn said.

The large Fang with the pale eyes, the one she seemed to gravitate to the most, made hand gestures ... Sign language, that was what it was called.

The dark-eyed Fang shook his head in disgust. "You would say that. *Let her do this her way.* You give her too much space, too much control. Right now, what she needs is someone else to take the reins and tell her what to do. Right now, she needs a wake-up call. She needs an injection of faith." He made for the door, but the pale-eyed Fang, Ash, that was it, intercepted him.

Tension rippled in the air.

"Ash, Logan, come on," Jace said.

"Let them have it out," the djinn said. "It's been coming for a while. They need to blow off the steam."

"Ash ..." Jace placed a hand on Ash's arm, obviously not on board with Sage's plan, and the big guy backed off.

Ash's body language screamed reluctance, though, and the steel in his eyes said he was a hair-breadth from changing his mind.

"Talk to her," Jace said to Logan. "If you think it will help."

Logan stormed from the room.

Ash began to pace, his body rippling as he moved. He'd been hard to shrug off when he'd tried to pin me in the tent. Out of them all, he was probably closest to me in strength; the djinn was also a close second. He was watching me now with his fiery gaze.

"What?"

"You're attracted to her, aren't you?" Sage said.

My blood turned to ice, because until that moment I'd been deliberately oblivious to that fact, but now… Fuck.

The djinn smiled. "It's the only reason you're not dead."

"Oh, and you think you could take me?"

He smiled, slow and wicked. "I wouldn't be alone."

Ash was glaring at me now, his arms crossed over his chest, and Jace was staring at me with open curiosity. Sage watched with evident glee. The bastard. He was enjoying this, but he couldn't know the truth, not yet, not until I'd confirmed it.

"She's a formidable woman." I smiled thinly and shrugged. "There's a sense of power about her, and now, with her origins revealed, it makes sense. Yes, there is an attraction I guess."

Ash signed something.

Sage chuckled. "He says if you touch her without her permission he'll rip your arms off."

I met Ash's eyes. He actually believed he'd be able to. I guess love made lions out of men. "I'm sure if I touched Eva without her permission she'd chop my hands off herself. There'd be no need for anyone else to do it."

Ash's eyes narrowed, and then he inclined his head, short and sharp.

The door behind us opened and Logan strode back into the lab, but he didn't come alone, he brought with him the scent of sex and Eva. My stomach clenched, and a growl vibrated in my chest. It was purely involuntary and shocking. I bit it back, but Ash had no such qualms; his eyes narrowed to slits, and he lunged at Logan. Jace made a grab for the big guy, but it was too late. Ash was across the room and on Logan in a blur. Fists flew, resulting in thuds and grunts and colorful curses from Logan.

Sage shook his head slowly and then stepped into the fray to pull Logan out from beneath an enraged Ash. The dark-haired Fang's lip was bleeding, and Ash's cheekbone was red. But the wounds would heal soon; they were, after all, Fangs.

Logan straightened his clothes. "You don't own her, Ash, and you know it. She wanted me."

Ash signed, his movements jerky with anger.

Logan's jaw ticked. "That's none of your fucking business. I'm going to get some air." He strode off toward the lift.

Ash yanked open the door to the cabins and disappeared.

I looked to Jace. "What did Ash say?"

Jace exhaled through his nose. "He asked Logan if Logan wanted Eva too. He asked him if he cared." Jace pinched the bridge of his nose. "I'm gonna go lie down."

He followed Ash out of the lab.

Sage turned to me. "Looks like it's just you and me. Since Eva seems to have recruited you as part of the team, maybe we should get better acquainted."

There was no slyness in the request; in fact, he looked more resigned than anything else.

Dammit. I'd wanted to speak to Jamie, but it looked like my chat with the scientist would have to wait.

I'D FINALLY MANAGED to shake Sage and make my way to Jamie's small lab. The scientist didn't even hear me enter his private domain. He was hunched over a microscope, muttering to himself. I cleared my throat, and he sat back with a start.

"Oh, um, hello? Can I help you?" he said.

I smiled, my pulse pounding a little too hard. "I need to know something."

"Of course, what is it?"

"The Vladul gene ... Where did you get that?"

Chapter Twenty-Nine

Hot water sluiced off my body, washing Logan's scent away. But it couldn't wash away the memory of him inside me or his words. There were no spare clothes here, but there was an oversized bathrobe. Slipping it on, I went back into the bedroom to find Ash sitting on the edge of my bed. His face was set in harsh lines, and his eyes were stormy. A bruise bloomed high on his cheekbone.

"Shit, Ash?" I knelt between his knees and peered up into his face. "Logan?"

He nodded and held up a scraped fist. Yeah, he'd given as good as he'd gotten— probably better, to be honest. His fist uncurled against my cheek to cup it, his other hand settled at the nape of my neck, massaging gently. His gaze was enquiring as it scanned my features.

"I'm okay."

He sighed and pressed a kiss to my forehead.

"I had sex with Logan." The words just tumbled out. "But I guess you know that."

His hand tightened a fraction on the back of my neck and then he pressed a kiss to my cheek.

My throat pinched. "I don't know what I'm doing right now, Ash. But in that moment, I wanted him. I think … there's a part of me that's wanted him for a while now."

His gray eyes were warm with understanding. He carefully pulled me up and onto his lap.

God, I didn't deserve him. He was kindness and safety and warmth, and there was no lying to him, not about anything. "Ash … I don't want to die."

He held me tighter, cradling me in his arms.

"I really, really don't." The dam I'd erected cracked and my vision blurred. "I'm scared, Ash. I'm so scared."

He rolled us onto the bed and wrapped himself around me. His breath was even and comforting, his hand soothing as I allowed the tsunami of fear to wash over me.

It lasted minutes, but it felt like hours, and when it was over my soul felt bruised and battered. Ash leaned over me, his face determined, his eyes blazing with conviction.

That's it, that look said. *You've purged the fear, now we get up and we fight. We find a solution. We find a way.* I buried my head in his shoulder and inhaled his scent before reluctantly pulling back.

"Let's go check on Jamie's progress."

His smile was filled with pride.

THE CURE WAS ALMOST READY, and everyone was locked away in their cabins getting some rest. Not me, though. With my days numbered, I needed to understand what I was, how I worked, and what was happening inside me if we were ever to find a way to stop it. Jamie had provided me with all the data, and I'd ignored the pitying look in his eyes. He didn't know me. He didn't know the world outside. He had no idea what I was capable of. He had no idea what the scientists at the Foundation could do.

Yes, Elias had filled me in about the advanced systems they had. There was hope.

There had to be.

Logan hadn't surfaced, so our paths hadn't crossed. Thank goodness, because I wasn't ready to look into his eyes and see indifference again. Instead, I stared at the data on the holo-screen. My genetic makeup, the notes, and the work leading up to my creation scrolled across the surface. Noah had screened my blood when we'd met, but he'd been looking only for the virus, he hadn't been looking at my DNA. On the surface, my blood looked human. Normal. What would he think of me now? If anyone could understand what it felt like to be different, it was the guys.

Jace had tried contacting Noah twice, but there'd been no response. It was worrying, but there was nothing we could do from here. Right now, the priority had to be the cure. We'd be back at the bunker soon enough.

I sensed Sage's presence as soon as he entered the room.

"This explains a lot," Sage said softly from behind me.

"Your ignited heart?" My mouth twisted wryly. "Yes, the percentage of djinn is quite high."

"Not as high as the Vladul and the fey." He studied the data. "But not only that, it explains why your blood is so intoxicating to the Fangs. A long time ago, Fangs would feed on fey as an aphrodisiac, but a treaty between the races put a stop to that after a psychotic Fang went on a killing spree targeting fey children. War was prevented when the insane Fang was handed over to the fey nobility and an enchanted treaty was signed."

Everything he was saying reinforced Jamie's warning, that the stabilizing marker was breaking down. My fey side was shining through in the taste of my blood, and the djinn side had broken through to ignite Sage's heart. I was devolving, or whatever the fuck it was called.

Sage's gaze was warm on the side of my face. There was more he wanted to say, and I could sense he was holding back.

I sighed and turned my head to lock gazes with him. "Sage, if there's something you want to say, then now is the time. Just ... say it."

His chest heaved in a hearty sigh. "I can't lose you." He pressed his lips together as if to cut off any further words.

He was powerful, he was otherworldly, and he was looking at me as if I was woven from magic and starlight.

My chest tightened. "Sage ..."

"Fuck it." He cupped my face in his huge hands. "You ignited my heart and that means something. That's a connection I won't lose. Of all the djinn DNA in all the world, you were woven with the spark that was meant to burn alongside mine. There has to be a way to save you, and I vow to you now that I will find it. I'll find it, or I will burn alongside you."

There was powerful sincerity in his words that

slammed into my heart and squeezed my lungs. A new heat bloomed behind my eyes, and my vision blurred. No. No more tears. I blinked them back.

"Trust me, I don't want to die, Sage."

He crushed me against him. "Then you won't. You fucking won't."

Logan and Ash had driven me to hope again, but in that moment, I truly believed that I could beat this. In that moment, I believed that I could somehow thwart my fate.

Faith is half the battle, Eva, Tobias whispered in my ear.

Yes, faith was half the battle, and I had my guys to make up the other half.

Chapter Thirty
ALPHA X (TOBIAS)

Color, sound, smells. I know these. They are familiar, as is the face staring at me. A female. My creator. Behind her stands my general. I am awake, alert and yet disconnected.

"Are we ready?" the male asks.

"We are," the female replies.

"Do it."

"Alpha X activated."

Letters scroll into my vision, green in color. They are important, they mean the world, and with them comes full sensation.

Mission objective: Eradication of all non-Fang supernatural signatures.

Mission status: Active.

To be continued…

Join Eva in *For the Reign*, the thrilling climax in the For the Blood Series.
Grab your copy of *For the Reign* now!

Chapter 1

I was burning up from the inside out, the world was a haze through my half open lids, and Ash's concerned face hovered over me. His hands, blessedly cool, skimmed my skin. I moaned and arched into his touch.

"Make it stop. Please." My words were a dry whisper.

"Fuck."

Logan?

"Get a cold compress and someone find Jeremy, now!" Logan ordered.

"I'll get Jeremy," Jace said.

What were they all doing in my room?

Where was I?

The genesis lab in the mountains … That was right. The vaccine … Jeremy, my dad's clone, was making the vaccine for us. I'd been sleeping, and now I was awake and on fire.

Ash's cool fingers soothed my fevered brow, and his soft lips pressed to my forehead.

"Out of the way." Logan's tone was terse.

Ash's cedar scent drifted away, and Logan's vanilla aroma replaced it. Something deliciously cool laved my forehead, my cheeks and my neck. Oh, God. Thank God. It drifted down to my chest and over my collar bones.

"More."

"Take her clothes off," Logan said.

Ash growled.

I forced my eyes open, to see their blurry forms facing off, and then closed them again.

A soft moan of protest rose from my lips. "Please."

Ash's hands were on me now, lifting me, peeling my sweat soaked clothes from my skin. Chilled air kissed my abdomen and then my chest.

"Motherfucker." Logan's word was a gasp. "Ash, what the fuck?"

"Djinn fire," Sage said. "It's her flame, but her human body isn't equipped to deal with it."

"Do something," Logan demanded.

"Give her to me," Sage said.

My half-dressed body was lifted, and then thick, powerful arms cradled me.

"Eva, can you hear me?" Sage's tone was gentle and coaxing.

My response was a strangled moan. Damn it, damn my swollen tongue and my tight throat.

"It's okay. I have you," he said.

His body was too warm, and I squirmed, trying to get away.

"No. trust me. You need to relax. You need to ride it. If you fight, it will consume you. Let me help you. Let me take some of your burden."

Ride it? It would kill me. It would incinerate me.

His lips brushed my ear. "Trust me *Habibata*. Trust me, my love."

Where his body was warm, his breath was cool, and my muscles relaxed a fraction.

"That's it," he said.

He sat, holding me on his lap, his powerful thighs taut beneath me. "I'm going to touch you now, and it may hurt, but only for a moment. Do not fight."

"You sure you know what you're doing?" Logan asked.

"As sure as I can be." Sage's tone was laced with anxiety.

His hand pressed against my breastbone, covering the strip of fabric holding my bra cups together, and then the fire inside me surged upward, burning and scraping. Pain. My back arched, and a scream ripped its way from my throat.

"Hush. Hush." He pressed harder, as if both drawing out the fire and pushing it down.

I was blind, mute, and trapped in an inferno. Stop. Please, stop. And like a prayer answered, I was free. A raw sob broke from my throat as the heat in my veins abated leaving me shaking and shivering.

Sage gathered me close, and then a blanket was wrapped around me, and my head was tucked under his chin.

"It's okay. You're going to be okay." The djinn rocked me, and his steady heartbeat soothed away the shakes.

"What is it?" Jeremy's voice—so like my father's —cut through the silence.

"You took your time," Logan snapped.

"I'm … I'm sorry."

I raised my head and cracked open my eyes. "This isn't his fault."

"Of course it's his fucking fault," Logan said. "He did this to you. Him and the human you call a father."

Logan's face was contorted in anger, but I couldn't summon any of my own to match it.

Instead, I allowed my eyes to drift closed again. "I just need a minute. I'm so tired."

"She was burning up," Sage said. "Djinn fire. I managed to help her control it."

"Then it has begun," Jeremy said softly. "I'll take another sample of blood. See what's—"

"No." I turned my face into Sage's chest, lips grazing the velvet skin exposed by the deep V of his tunic. "No more samples, no more tests. I'm dying, and I'll be damned if I'll waste any more time where nothing can be done about it. We have a foundation to infiltrate and a cure to distribute, and I'm not ready to die." I turned my face to the guys, my jaw clenched. "Not for a long time."

Logan's dark eyes gleamed in triumph, and Ash pressed his lips together and signed something fast and urgent.

Jace nodded. "I'll rally Kira and her guys."

I smiled at the fang, and his cheeks reddened. "Thank you."

"We'll be out in a minute," Sage said.

Ash's eyes narrowed and locked on mine. He was checking if I was okay with this arrangement because it was usually Ash that did the comforting, but right now, with the djinn fire raging within, Sage was the most qualified to help me.

"I'll be fine." I met Ash's gaze, pouring my love into that one look.

He inclined his head and headed for the door,

and the others followed, leaving me alone with the djinn.

Sage pulled the blanket tighter around me and then kissed the top of my head. "How are you feeling now?"

"Cold."

He tilted my chin with the crook of his finger and leaned in so that our lips were a mere hairbreadth apart.

"I can warm you up, if you like?"

The pulse at the base of my throat thudded hard. "I'd like."

He brushed his lips over mine once, twice, causing my pulse to flutter and throb, and then he kissed my top lip, and gently sucked on my bottom lip, but damn, I wanted more. I needed more. I wound my arm around his neck and pulled him close. It was my turn to claim. I sucked his bottom lip into my mouth and then drew back slowly, grazing his lip between my teeth with just the right pressure to elicit a sexy growl.

"Damn it, Eva, do you want to burn?"

I pulled back enough to look into the maelstrom of fiery colors in his eyes. "This kind of burn I can handle." I kissed him hard on the mouth. "This kind of burn I want."

His hand slid up my back, brushing along my

spine, and then cupped my nape. "Eva, Eva, the things I would do to you ..."

And then he ducked his head to kiss my neck, to suck and lick across my collar bones and down to the rise of my breasts. His free hand cupped me, massaging me until my nipples were painfully hard and the juncture of my thighs was pounding, desperate and wet, and then he pulled down my bra and closed his mouth over my aching nipple. My cry was reedy and breathless, and his moan of satisfaction inflamed my desire.

"Sage, God. Don't stop."

But he did. He slowly pulled away, and carefully adjusted my bra to cover me. The blanket was pulled up next, and then he hugged me close.

"When I take you, it won't be rushed, and it won't be like this." He pressed his forehead to mine. "You're too special for that."

A lump formed in my throat. "I guess then we should get going?"

He chuckled low and enticing. "Yes, Eva. We should."

LOGAN, Jace, Ash and Jeremy were in the lab when Sage and I emerged a few minutes later. I'd changed back into the clothes Kira had loaned me, and my sheath and tulwar were gripped in my hand.

Jeremy was fiddling with something at one of the counters while Logan and Jace watched. Ash was leaning on another counter behind the scientist, but his gaze shot up to meet mine as soon as I entered.

"Are we ready?" My question was directed at Jeremy, but it was Logan who answered.

"Yeah. He's done."

"And the others? Where are they? Where's Elias?"

"Outside," Jace said.

"You left Elias with Kira's guys?"

Logan arched a brow. "I doubt Bates will try anything with Elias, not after you tore him a new one the last time. Besides, I don't think Elias will simply stand back and get knocked about this time."

He had a point.

Jeremy held up a black pouch and unzipped it to reveal four vials, each the size of my thumb. The vials contained a clear liquid.

"Two to combat the original virus and two for the mutated one," Jeremy said. "I've labeled them."

He carefully zipped up the padded pouch, which also had a waist strap, and handed it to me. This was our hope. This was the future and it was in my hands, and then it was strapped to my waist.

"We're good to go," Jace said. "Kira said they have enough fuel to get us back to our bunker, back to Noah. It'll take us at least fifteen hours, and we'll take shifts to drive. She's already been on the radio to Nathanial. He's rallying the troops and has sent an emissary to the two fang broods that they've been in contact with."

I nodded. "Good. Do we have a rendezvous point?"

"My camp," Sage said. "We meet up at my camp in three days' time. It should be long enough for everyone to make the journey, and the wards will protect us all while we plan our attack."

It was early, just gone six am, so if we were lucky, we'd be home before sunset.

Home.

Weird, as I'd only lived there for a couple of days, but still. "Have you managed to get hold of Noah?"

Jace's expression was somber. "No."

"It's worrying," Logan said.

It was but worrying about it would be a waste of time. We couldn't do anything about it from here. "Well, then we best get back."

I had a month, maybe less, left before I unraveled. There was no wasting time.

"Good luck, Eva," Jeremy said softly. "Frederick would be so proud of you."

His smile was closed lipped, his eyes dull. We were about to leave him alone once more. He'd been trapped here all his life. A clone, a thing to be used just like me. Frederick, the man I'd called father, had created him and then abandoned him here to wait for me. To wait until it was time to synthesize the cure, and he had done so. Faithful and diligent till the end. All those years alone. It didn't bear thinking about. But no more.

"Well?" I cocked my head. "Are you coming?"

Jeremy blinked at me in surprise. "You … you want me to go with you?"

I shrugged. "Well, it looks like my dad left you here for a purpose, a purpose you've now fulfilled. So, yeah. If you want to, then you should come with us."

He opened and closed his mouth a couple of times. "I … I'll get my things." He hurried from the room, pausing once to glance over his shoulder with a shaky smile. "You'll wait?"

"Yes, Jeremy, we'll wait for you." Just like you waited for me.

He may be my dad's clone, but he was nothing like him. He was softer, wacky and he'd die in the outside world without someone to watch out for him.

"Are you sure about this?" Logan asked.

"I'm not leaving him here alone. No one deserves to be alone."

Logan pressed his lips together. "Okay. I'll go give him a hand, make sure he doesn't try to pack the whole damn lab to take with him."

He stomped off after Jeremy.

I looked to Ash who was locked in silent communication with Sage. They did this from time to time, and I'd never asked them what it was they were actually doing. Could Sage hear Ash? Did Ash have a voice in Sage's mind?

"Sometimes," Sage said to me.

"What?" I blinked up at him.

"You were wondering if I could hear Ash's thoughts, and the answer is sometimes I can. Especially when the thoughts are about your welfare." Sage smiled. "That's when he speaks the loudest."

Ash's throat bobbed, and I stepped up to him and wrapped my arms around his chest. "I'm fine. I'm going to be fine."

He hugged me back and kissed the top of my head.

Sage headed for the lift. "I'm surprised you didn't ask about it before, Miss inquisitive."

Ash and I followed. "If you hadn't noticed, I've had a lot on my plate recently. Fighting Feral, trying to stay alive, fighting Feral ... Oh, yeah, trying to stay alive ..."

He chuckled as we stepped into the lift together. "Well, we're almost there, Eva. We're almost there."

Almost but there was still a way to go. The sooner we got home and collected Noah, the sooner we could get to camp and start the final stretch of our journey.

Grab your copy of *For the Reign* now!

Other books by Debbie Cassidy

The Gatekeeper Chronicles

Coauthored with Jasmine Walt

Marked by Sin

Hunted by Sin

Claimed by Sin

The Witch Blood Chronicles

(Spin-off to the Gatekeeper Chronicles)

Binding Magick

Defying Magick

Embracing Magick

Unleashing Magick

The Fearless Destiny Series

Beyond Everlight

Into Evernight

Under Twilight

The Chronicles of Midnight

Protector of Midnight

Champion of Midnight

Secrets of Midnight

Shades of Midnight

Savior of Midnight

Chronicles of Arcana

City of Demons

City of the Lost

City of the Everdark

City of War

For the Blood

For the Blood

For the Power

For the Reign

Heart of Darkness

Captive of Darkness

Bane of Winter

The Oblivion Heart

Novellas

Blood Blade

Grotesque – A Vampire Diary Kindle World book

About the Author

Debbie Cassidy lives in England, Bedfordshire, with her three kids and very supportive husband. Coffee and chocolate biscuits are her writing fuels of choice, and she is still working on getting that perfect tower of solitude built in her back garden. Obsessed with building new worlds and reading about them, she spends her spare time daydreaming and conversing with the characters in her head – in a totally non psychotic way of course. She writes High Fantasy and Urban Fantasy. Connect with Debbie via her website at debbiecassidyauthor.com or twitter @authordcassidy. Or sign up to her Newsletter to stay in the know.

Made in the USA
Columbia, SC
20 March 2023

14068640R00193